Maud Martha

Gwendolyn Brooks

Books by Gwendolyn Brooks

ANNIE ALLEN

A STREET IN BRONZEVILLE

MAUD MARTHA

Maud Martha

A NOVEL

by

GWENDOLYN BROOKS

Harper & Brothers, Publishers
New York

MAUD MARTHA

Printed in the United States of America

FIRST EDITION

I-C

Library of Congress catalog card number: 53–7726

To my family,

Henry, Henry, and Nora

CONTENTS

Maud Martha

1

description of Maud Martha

WHAT she liked was candy buttons, and books, and painted music (deep blue, or delicate silver) and the west sky, so altering, viewed from the steps of the back porch; and dandelions.

She would have liked a lotus, or China asters or the Japanese Iris, or meadow lilies—yes, she would have liked meadow lilies, because the very word meadow made her breathe more deeply, and either fling her arms or want to fling her arms, depending on who was by, rapturously up to whatever was watching in the sky. But dandelions were what she chiefly saw. Yellow jewels for everyday, studding the patched green dress of her back yard. She liked their demure prettiness second to their everydayness; for in that latter quality she thought she saw a picture of herself, and it was comforting to find that what was common could also be a flower.

And could be cherished! To be cherished was the dearest wish of the heart of Maud Martha Brown, and sometimes when she was not looking at dandelions (for one would not be looking at them all the time, often there were chairs and tables to dust or tomatoes to slice or beds to make or grocery stores to be gone to, and in the colder months there were no dandelions at all), it was hard to believe that a thing of only ordinary allurements—if the allurements of any flower could be said to be ordinary—was as easy to love as a thing of heart-catching beauty.

Such as her sister Helen! who was only two years past her own age of seven, and was almost her own height and weight and thickness. But oh, the long lashes, the grace, the little ways with the hands and feet.

2

spring landscape: detail

THE school looked solid. Brownish-red brick, dirty cream stone trim. Massive chimney, candid, serious. The sky was gray, but the sun was making little silver promises somewhere up there, hinting. A wind blew. What sort of June day was this? It was more like the last days of November. It was more than rather bleak; still, there were these little promises, just under cover; whether they would fulfill themselves was anybody's guess.

spring landscape: detail

Up the street, mixed in the wind, blew the children, and turned the corner onto the brownish-red brick school court. It was wonderful. Bits of pink, of blue, white, yellow, green, purple, brown, black, carried by jerky little stems of brown or yellow or brown-black, blew by the unhandsome gray and decay of the double-apartment buildings, past the little plots of dirt and scanty grass that held up their narrow brave banners: PLEASE KEEP OFF THE GRASS—NEWLY SEEDED. There were lives in the buildings. Past the tiny lives the children blew. Cramp, inhibition, choke—they did not trouble themselves about these. They spoke shrilly of ways to fix curls and pompadours, of "nasty" boys and "sharp" boys, of Joe Louis, of ice cream, of bicycles, of baseball, of teachers, of examinations, of Duke Ellington, of Bette Davis. They spoke—or at least Maud Martha spoke—of the sweet potato pie that would be served at home.

It was six minutes to nine; in one minute the last bell would ring. "Come on! You'll be late!" Low cries. A quickening of steps. A fluttering of brief cases. Inevitably, though, the fat girl, who was forced to be nonchalant, who pretended she little cared whether she was late or not, who would *not* run! (Because she would wobble, would lose her dignity.) And inevitably the little fellows in knickers, ten, twelve, thirteen years old, nonchalant just for the fun of it—who lingered on the red bricks, throwing balls to each other, or reading newspapers and comic books, or punching each other half playfully.

But eventually every bit of the wind managed to blow itself in, and by five minutes after nine the school court was bare. There was not a hot cap nor a bow ribbon anywhere.

3

love and gorillas

so the gorilla really did escape!

She was sure of it, now that she was awake. For she was awake. This was awakeness. Stretching, curling her fingers, she was still rather protected by the twists of thin smoky stuff from the too sudden onslaught of the red draperies with white and green flowers on them, and the picture of the mother and dog loving a baby, and the dresser with blue paper flowers on it. But that she was now awake in all earnest she could not doubt.

That train—a sort of double-deck bus affair, traveling in a blue-lined half dark. Slow, that traveling. Slow. More like a boat. It came to a stop before the gorilla's cage. The gorilla, lying back, his arms under his head, one leg resting casually across the other, watched the people. Then he rose, lumbered over to the door of his cage, peered, clawed at his bars, shook his bars. All the people on the lower deck climbed to the upper deck.

But why would they not get off?

"Motor trouble!" called the conductor. "Motor trouble! And the gorilla, they think, will escape!"

But why would not the people get off?

Then there was flaring green and there was red and there was red-orange, and she was in the middle of it, her few years many times added to, doubtless, for she was treated as an adult. All the people were afraid, but no one would get off.

All the people wondered if the gorilla would escape.

Awake, she knew he had.

She was safe, but the others—were they eaten? and if so had he begun on the heads first? and could he eat such things as buttons and watches and hair? or would he first tear those away?

Maud Martha got up, and on her way to the bathroom cast a glance toward her parents' partly open door. Her parents were close together. Her father's arm was around her mother.

Why, how lovely!

For she remembered last night. Her father stamping out grandly, dressed in his nicest suit and hat, and her mother left alone. Later, she and Helen and Harry had gone out with their mother for a "night hike."

How she loved a "hike." Especially in the evening, for then everything was moody, odd, deliciously threatening, always hunched and ready to close in on you but never doing so. East of Cottage Grove you saw fewer people, and those you did see had, all of them (how strange, thought Maud Martha), white faces. Over there that matter of mystery and hunchedness was thicker, a hundred-fold.

Shortly after they had come in, Daddy had too. The children had been sent to bed, and off Maud Martha had gone to her sleep and her gorilla. (Although she had not known that in the beginning, oh no!) In the deep deep night she had waked, just a little, and had called "Mama." Mama had said, "Shut up!"

The little girl did not mind being told harshly to shut up when her mother wanted it quiet so that she and Daddy could love each other.

Because she was very *very* happy that their quarrel was over and that they would once again be nice.

Even though while the loud hate or silent cold was going on, Mama was so terribly sweet and good to her.

4

death of Grandmother

THEY had to sit in a small lobby, waiting for the nurses to change Gramma.

"She can't control herself," explained Maud Martha's mother.

Oh what a thing! What a thing.

When finally they could be admitted, Belva Brown, Maud Martha and Harry tiptoed into the lackluster room, single file.

Gramma lay in what seemed to Maud Martha a wooden coffin. Boards had been put up on either side of the bed to keep the patient from harming herself. All the morning, a nurse confided, Ernestine Brown had been trying to get out of the bed and go home.

They looked in the coffin. Maud Martha felt sick. That was not her Gramma. Couldn't be. Elongated, pulpy-looking face. Closed eyes; lashes damp-appearing, heavy lids. Straight flat thin form under a dark gray blanket. And the voice thick and raw. "Hawh—hawh—hawh." Maud Martha was frightened. But she mustn't show it. She spoke to the semi-corpse.

"Hello, Gramma. This is Maudie." After a moment, "Do you know me, Gramma?"

"Hawh—"

"Do you feel better? Does anything hurt you?"

"Hawh—" Here Gramma slightly shook her head. She did not open her eyes, but apparently she could understand whatever they said. And maybe, thought Maud Martha, what we are not saying.

How alone they were, how removed from this

woman, this ordinary woman who had suddenly become a queen, for whom presently the most interesting door of them all would open, who, lying locked in boards with her "hawhs," yet towered, triumphed over them, while they stood there asking the stupid questions people ask the sick, out of awe, out of half horror, half envy.

"I never saw anybody die before," thought Maud Martha. "But I'm seeing somebody die now."

What was that smell? When would her mother go? She could not stand much more. What was that smell? She turned her gaze away for a while. To look at the other patients in the room, instead of at Gramma! The others were white women. There were three of them, two wizened ones, who were asleep, a stout woman of about sixty, who looked insane, and who was sitting up in bed, wailing, "Why don't they come and bring me a bedpan? Why don't they? Nobody brings me a bedpan." She clutched Maud Martha's coat hem, and stared up at her with glass-bright blue eyes, begging, "Will you tell them to bring me a bedpan? Will you?" Maud Martha promised, and the weak hand dropped.

"Poor dear," said the stout woman, glancing tenderly at Gramma.

When they finally left the room and the last "hawh," Maud Martha told a nurse passing down the hall just then about the woman who wanted the bedpan. The nurse tightened her lips. "Well, she can keep on wanting," she said, after a moment's indignant silence. "That's all they do, day long, night long—whine for the bedpan. We can't give them the bedpan every two minutes. Just forget it, Miss."

They started back down the long corridor. Maud Martha put her arm around her mother.

"Oh Mama," she whimpered, "she—she looked awful. I had no idea. I never saw such a horrible—creature—" A hard time she had, keeping the tears back. And as for her brother, Harry had not said a word since entering the hospital.

When they got back to the house, Papa was receiving a telephone message. Ernestine Brown was dead.

She who had taken the children of Abraham Brown to the circus, and who had bought them pink popcorn, and Peanut Crinkle candy, who had laughed—that Ernestine was dead.

5

you're being so good, so kind

MAUD MARTHA looked the living room over. Nicked old upright piano. Sag-seat leather arm-chair. Three or four straight chairs that had long ago given up the ghost of whatever shallow dignity they may have had in the beginning and looked completely disgusted with themselves and with the Brown family. Mantel with scroll decorations that usually seemed rather elegant but which since morning had become unspeakably vulgar, impossible.

There was a small hole in the sad-colored rug, near the sofa. Not an outrageous hole. But she shuddered. She dashed to the sofa, maneuvered it till the hole could not be seen.

She sniffed a couple of times. Often it was said that colored people's houses necessarily had a certain heavy, unpleasant smell. Nonsense, that was. Vicious—and nonsense. But she raised every window.

Here was the theory of racial equality about to be put into practice, and she only hoped she would be equal to being equal.

No matter how taut the terror, the fall proceeds to its dregs. . . .

At seven o'clock her heart was starting to make itself heard, and with great energy she was assuring herself that, though she liked Charles, though she admired Charles, it was only at the high school that she wanted to see Charles.

This was no Willie or Richard or Sylvester coming to call on her. Neither was she Charles's Sally or Joan. She was the whole "colored" race, and

Charles was the personalization of the entire Caucasian plan.

At three minutes to eight the bell rang, hesitantly. Charles! No doubt regretting his impulse already. No doubt regarding, with a rueful contempt, the outside of the house, so badly in need of paint. Those rickety steps. She retired into the bathroom. Presently she heard her father go to the door; her father—walking slowly, walking patiently, walking unafraid, as if about to let in a paper boy who wanted his twenty cents, or an insurance man, or Aunt Vivian, or no more than Woodette Williams, her own silly friend.

What was this she was feeling now? Not fear, not fear. A sort of gratitude! It sickened her to realize it. As though Charles, in coming, gave her a gift.

Recipient and benefactor.

It's so good of you.

You're being so good.

6

at the Regal

THE applause was quick. And the silence—final.

That was what Maud Martha, sixteen and very erect, believed, as she manipulated herself through a heavy outflowing crowd in the lobby of the Regal Theatre on Forty-seventh and South Park.

She thought of fame, and of that singer, that Howie Joe Jones, that tall oily brown thing with hair set in thickly pomaded waves, with cocky teeth, eyes like thin glass. With—a Voice. A Voice that Howie Joe's publicity described as "rugged honey." She had not been favorably impressed. She had not been able to thrill. Not even when he threw his head back so that his waves dropped low, shut his eyes sweetly, writhed, thrust out his arms (really *gave* them to the world) and thundered out, with passionate seriousness, with deep meaning, with high purpose—

—Sa-WEET sa-OOOO
Jaust-a YOOOOOOO—

Maud Martha's brow wrinkled. The audience had applauded. Had stamped its strange, hilarious foot. Had put its fingers in its mouth—whistled. Had sped a shininess up to its eyes. But now part of it was going home, as she was, and its face was dull again. It had not been helped. Not truly. Not well. For a hot half hour it had put that light gauze across its little miseries and monotonies, but now here they were again, ungauzed, self-assertive, cancerous as ever. The audience had gotten a fairy gold. And it was not going to spend the rest of its life, or even the rest of the night, being grateful to Howie Joe Jones. No, it would not make plans to raise a hard monument to him.

She swung out of the lobby, turned north.

The applause was quick.

But the silence was final, so what was the singer's profit?

Money.

You had to admit Howie Joe Jones was making money. Money that was raced to the track, to the De Lisa, to women, to the sellers of cars; to Capper and Capper, to Henry C. Lytton and Company for those suits in which he looked like an upright corpse. She read all about it in the columns of the Chicago *Defender's* gossip departments.

She had never understood how people could parade themselves on a stage like that, exhibit their precious private identities; shake themselves about; be very foolish for a thousand eyes.

She was going to keep herself to herself. She did not want fame. She did not want to be a "star."

To create—a role, a poem, picture, music, a rapture in stone: great. But not for her.

What she wanted was to donate to the world a good Maud Martha. That was the offering, the bit of art, that could not come from any other.

She would polish and hone that.

7

Tim

OH, how he used to wriggle!—do little mean things! do great big wonderful things! and laugh laugh laugh.

He had shaved and he had scratched himself through the pants. He had lain down and ached for want of a woman. He had married. He had wiped out his nostrils with bits of tissue paper in the presence of his wife and his wife had turned her head, quickly, but politely, to avoid seeing them as they dropped softly into the toilet, and floated. He had had a big stomach and an alarmingly loud laugh. He had been easy with the ain'ts and sho-nuffs. He had been drunk one time, only one time, and on that occasion had done the Charleston in the middle of what was then Grand Boulevard and is now South Park, at four in the morning. Here was a man who had absorbed the headlines in the *Tribune,* studied the cartoons in *Collier's* and the *Saturday Evening Post.*

These facts she had known about her Uncle Tim. And she had known that he liked sweet potato pie. But what were the facts that she had not known, that his wife, her father's sister Nannie, had not known? The things that nobody had known.

Maud Martha looked down at the gray clay lying hard-lipped, cold, definitely not about to rise and punch off any alarm clock, on the tufted white satin that was at once so beautiful and so ghastly. I must tell them, she thought, as she walked back to her seat, I must let Helen and Harry know how

I want to be arranged in my casket; I don't want my head straight up like that; I want my head turned a little to the right, so my best profile will be showing; and I want my left hand resting on my breast, nicely; and I want my hair plain, not waved—I don't want to look like a gray clay doll.

It all came down to gray clay.

Then just what was important? What had been important about this life, this Uncle Tim? Was the world any better off for his having lived? A little, perhaps. Perhaps he had stopped his car short once, and saved a dog, so that another car could kill it a month later. Perhaps he had given some little street wretch a nickel's worth of peanuts in its unhappy hour, and that little wretch would grow up and forget Uncle Tim but all its life would carry in its heart an anonymous, seemingly underivative softness for mankind. Perhaps. Certainly he had been good to his wife Nannie. She had never said a word against him.

But how important was this, what was the real importance of this, what would—God say? Oh, no! What she would rather mean was, what would Uncle Tim say, if he could get back?

Maud Martha looked at Aunt Nannie. Aunt Nannie had put too much white powder on her face. Was it irreverent, Maud Martha wondered, to be able to think of powdering your face for a funeral, when you were the new widow? Not in this case, she decided, for (she remembered this other thing about him) Uncle Tim, whose nose was always oily, had disliked an oily nose. Aunt Nannie was being brave. As yet she had not dropped a tear. But then, her turn at the casket had not come.

A large woman in a white uniform and white stockings and low-heeled white shoes was playing "We Shall Understand It Better By and By" at the organ, almost inaudibly (with a little jazz roll in her bass). How gentle the music was, how suggestive. Maud Martha saw people, after having all but knocked themselves out below, climbing up the golden, golden stairs, to a throne where sat Jesus, or the Almighty God; who promptly opened a

Book, similar to the arithmetic book she had had in grammar school, turned to the back, and pointed out—the Answers! And the people, poor little things, nodding and cackling among themselves—"So that was it all the time! that is what I should have done!" "But—so simple! so *easy!* I should just have turned here! instead of there!" How wonderful! Was it true? Were people to get the Answers in the sky? Were people really going to understand It better by and by? When it was too late?

8

home

WHAT had been wanted was this always, this always to last, the talking softly on this porch, with the snake plant in the jardiniere in the southwest corner, and the obstinate slip from Aunt Eppie's magnificent Michigan fern at the left side of the friendly door. Mama, Maud Martha and Helen rocked slowly in their rocking chairs, and looked at the late afternoon light on the lawn, and at the emphatic iron of the fence and at the poplar tree.

These things might soon be theirs no longer. Those shafts and pools of light, the tree, the graceful iron, might soon be viewed possessively by different eyes.

Papa was to have gone that noon, during his lunch hour, to the office of the Home Owners' Loan. If he had not succeeded in getting another extension, they would be leaving this house in which they had lived for more than fourteen years. There was little hope. The Home Owners' Loan was hard. They sat, making their plans.

"We'll be moving into a nice flat somewhere," said Mama. "Somewhere on South Park, or Michigan, or in Washington Park Court." Those flats, as the girls and Mama knew well, were burdens on wages twice the size of Papa's. This was not mentioned now.

"They're much prettier than this old house," said Helen. "I have friends I'd just as soon not bring here. And I have other friends that wouldn't come down this far for anything, unless they were in a taxi."

Yesterday, Maud Martha would have attacked

her. Tomorrow she might. Today she said nothing. She merely gazed at a little hopping robin in the tree, her tree, and tried to keep the fronts of her eyes dry.

"Well, I do know," said Mama, turning her hands over and over, "that I've been getting tireder and tireder of doing that firing. From October to April, there's firing to be done."

"But lately we've been helping, Harry and I," said Maud Martha. "And sometimes in March and April and in October, and even in November, we could build a little fire in the fireplace. Sometimes the weather was just right for that."

She knew, from the way they looked at her, that this had been a mistake. They did not want to cry.

But she felt that the little line of white, somewhat ridged with smoked purple, and all that cream-shot saffron, would never drift across any western sky except that in back of this house. The rain would drum with as sweet a dullness nowhere but here. The birds on South Park were mechanical birds, no better than the poor caught canaries in those "rich" women's sun parlors.

"It's just going to kill Papa!" burst out Maud Martha. "He loves this house! He *lives* for this house!"

"He lives for us," said Helen. "It's us he loves. He wouldn't want the house, except for us."

"And he'll have us," added Mama, "wherever."

"You know," Helen sighed, "if you want to know the truth, this is a relief. If this hadn't come up, we would have gone on, just dragged on, hanging out here forever."

"It might," allowed Mama, "be an act of God. God may just have reached down, and picked up the reins."

"Yes," Maud Martha cracked in, "that's what you always say—that God knows best."

Her mother looked at her quickly, decided the statement was not suspect, looked away.

Helen saw Papa coming. "There's Papa," said Helen.

They could not tell a thing from the way Papa

was walking. It was that same dear little staccato walk, one shoulder down, then the other, then repeat, and repeat. They watched his progress. He passed the Kennedys', he passed the vacant lot, he passed Mrs. Blakemore's. They wanted to hurl themselves over the fence, into the street, and shake the truth out of his collar. He opened his gate—the gate—and still his stride and face told them nothing.

"Hello," he said.

Mama got up and followed him through the front door. The girls knew better than to go in too.

Presently Mama's head emerged. Her eyes were lamps turned on.

"It's all right," she exclaimed. "He got it. It's all over. Everything is all right."

The door slammed shut. Mama's footsteps hurried away.

"I think," said Helen, rocking rapidly, "I think I'll give a party. I haven't given a party since I was eleven. I'd like some of my friends to just casually see that we're homeowners."

9

Helen

WHAT she remembered was Emmanuel; laughing, glinting in the sun; kneeing his wagon toward them, as they walked tardily home from school. Six years ago.

"How about a ride?" Emmanuel had hailed.

She had, daringly—it was not her way, not her native way—made a quip. A "sophisticated" quip. "Hi, handsome!" Instantly he had scowled, his dark face darkening.

"I don't mean you, you old black gal," little Emmanuel had exclaimed. "I mean Helen."

He had meant Helen, and Helen on the reissue of the invitation had climbed, without a word, into the wagon and was off and away.

Even now, at seventeen—high school graduate, mistress of her fate, and a ten-dollar-a-week file clerk in the very Forty-seventh Street lawyer's office where Helen was a fifteen-dollar-a-week typist—as she sat on Helen's bed and watched Helen primp for a party, the memory hurt. There was no consolation in the thought that not now and not then would she have *had* Emmanuel "off a Christmas tree." For the basic situation had never changed. Helen was still the one they wanted in the wagon, still "the pretty one," "the dainty one." The lovely one.

She did not know what it was. She had tried to find the something that must be there to imitate, that she might imitate it. But she did not know what it was. I wash as much as Helen does, she thought. My hair is longer and thicker, she thought. I'm much smarter. I read books and newspapers and old folks like to talk with me, she thought.

But the kernel of the matter was that, in spite of these things, she was poor, and Helen was still the ranking queen, not only with the Emmanuels of the world, but even with their father—their mother—their brother. She did not blame the family. It was not their fault. She understood. They could not help it. They were enslaved, were fascinated, and they were not at all to blame.

Her noble understanding of their blamelessness did not make any easier to bear such a circumstance as Harry's springing to open a door so that Helen's soft little hands might not have to cope with the sullyings of a doorknob, or running her errands, to save the sweet and fine little feet, or shouldering Helen's part against Maud Martha. Especially could these items burn when Maud Martha recalled her comradely rompings with Harry, watched by the gentle Helen from the clean and gentle harbor of the porch: take the day, for example, when Harry had been chased by those five big boys from Forty-first and Wabash, cursing, smelling, beastlike boys! with bats and rocks, and little stones that were more worrying than rocks; on that occasion out Maud Martha had dashed, when she saw from the front-room window Harry, panting and torn, racing for home; out she had dashed and down into the street with one of the smaller porch chairs held high over her head, and while Harry gained first the porch and next the safety side of the front door she had swung left, swung right, clouting a head here, a head there, and screaming at the top of her lungs, "Y' leave my brother alone! Y' leave my brother alone!" And who had washed those bloody wounds, and afterward vaselined them down? Really—in spite of everything she could not understand why Harry had to hold open doors for Helen, and calmly let them slam in her, Maud Martha's, his friend's, face.

It did not please her either, at the breakfast table, to watch her father drink his coffee and contentedly think (oh, she knew it!), as Helen started on her grapefruit, how daintily she ate, how gracefully she sat in her chair, how pure was her robe and unwrinkled, how neatly she had arranged her hair. Their father preferred Helen's hair to Maud Martha's (Maud Martha knew), which impressed him, not with its length and body, but simply with its apparent untamableness; for he would never get over that zeal of his for order in all things, in character, in housekeeping, in his own labor, in grooming, in human relationships. Always he had worried about Helen's homework, Helen's health. And now that boys were taking her out, he believed not one of them worthy of her, not one of them good enough to receive a note of her sweet voice: he insisted that she be returned before midnight. Yet who was it who sympathized with him in his decision to remain, for the rest of his days, the simple janitor! when everyone else was urging him to get out, get prestige, make more money? Who was it who sympathized with him in his almost desperate love for this old house? Who followed him about, emotionally speaking, loving this, doting on that? The kitchen, for instance, that was not beautiful in any way! The walls and ceilings, that were cracked. The chairs, which cried when people sat in them. The tables, that grieved audibly if anyone rested more than two fingers upon them. The huge cabinets, old and tired (when you shut their doors or drawers there was a sick, bickering little sound). The radiators, high and hideous. And underneath the low sink coiled unlovely pipes, that Helen said made her think of a careless woman's underwear, peeping out. In fact, often had Helen given her opinion, unasked, of the whole house, of the whole "hulk of rotten wood." Often had her cool and gentle eyes sneered, gently and coolly, at her father's determination to hold his poor estate. But take that kitchen, for instance! Maud Martha, taking it, saw herself there, up and down her seventeen years, eating apples after school; making sweet potato tarts; drawing, on the pathetic table, the horse that won her the sixth grade prize; getting her hair curled for her first party, at that stove; washing dishes by summer twilight, with the back door wide open; making cheese and peanut butter sandwiches for a picnic. And even crying, crying in that pantry, when no one knew. The old sorrows brought there!—now dried, flattened out, breaking into interesting dust at the merest look. . . .

"You'll never get a boy friend," said Helen, fluffing on her Golden Peacock powder, "if you don't stop reading those books."

10

first beau

HE had a way of putting his hands on a Woman. Light, but perforating. Passing by, he would touch the Woman's hair, he would give the Woman's hair a careless, and yet deliberate, caress, working down from the top to the ends, then gliding to the chin, then lifting the chin till the poor female's eyes were forced to meet his, then proceeding down the neck. Maud Martha had watched this technique time after time, privately swearing that if he ever tried it on her she would settle him soon enough. Finally he had tried it, and a sloppy feeling had filled her, and she had not settled him at all. Not that she was thereafter, like the others, his to command, flatter, neglect, swing high, swing low, smooth with a grin, wrinkle with a scowl, just as his fancy wished. For Russell lacked—what? He was—nice. He was fun to go about with. He was decorated inside and out. He did things, said things, with a flourish. That was what he was. He was a flourish. He was a dazzling, long, and sleepily swishing flourish. "He will never be great," Maud Martha thought. "But he wouldn't be hurt if anybody told him that—if possible to choose from two, he would without hesitation choose being grand."

There he sat before her, in a sleeveless yellow-tan sweater and white, open-collared sport shirt, one leg thrust sexily out, fist on that hip, brown eyes ablaze, chin thrust up at her entrance as if *it* were to give her greeting, devil-like smile making her blink.

11

second beau

AND—don't laugh—he wanted a dog.

A picture of the English country gentleman. Roaming the rustic hill. He had not yet bought a pipe. He would immediately.

There already was the herringbone tweed. (Although old sensuousness, old emotional daring broke out at the top of the trousers, where there was that gathering, that kicked-back yearning toward the pleat!) There was the tie a man might think about for an hour before entering that better shop, in order to be able to deliberate only a sharp two minutes at the counter, under the icy estimate of the salesman. Here were the socks, here was the haircut, here were the shoes. The educated smile, the slight bow, the faint imperious nod. He belonged to the world of the university.

He was taking a number of loose courses on the Midway.

His scent was withdrawn, expensive, as he strode down the worn carpet of her living room, as though it were the educated green of the Midway.

He considered Parrington's *Main Currents in American Thought*. He had not mastered it. Only recently, he announced, had he learned of its existence. "Three volumes of the most reasonable approaches!—Yet there are chaps on that campus—*young!*—younger than I am—who read it years ago, who know it, who have had it for themselves for years, who have been seeing it on their fathers' shelves since infancy. They heard it discussed at the dinner table when they were four. As a ball is to me, so Parrington is to them. They've been kicking him around for years, like a *foot*ball!"

The idea agitated. His mother had taken in washing. She had had three boys, whom she sent to school clean but patched-up. Just so they were clean, she had said. That was all that mattered, she had said. She had said "ain't." She had said, "I ain't stud'n you." His father—he hadn't said anything at all.

He himself had had a paper route. Had washed windows, cleaned basements, sanded furniture, shoveled snow, hauled out trash and garbage for the neighbors. He had worked before that, running errands for people when he was six. What chance did he have, he mused, what chance was there for anybody coming out of a set of conditions that never allowed for the prevalence of sensitive, and intellectual, yet almost frivolous, dinner-table discussions of Parrington across four-year-old heads?

Whenever he left the Midway, said David McKemster, he was instantly depressed. East of Cottage Grove, people were clean, going somewhere that mattered, not talking unless they had something to say. West of the Midway, they leaned against buildings and their mouths were opening and closing very fast but nothing important was coming out. What did they know about Aristotle? The unhappiness he felt over there was physical. He wanted to throw up. There was a fence on Forty-seventh and—Champlain? Langley? Forestville?—he forgot what; broken, rotten, trying to lie down; and passing it on a windy night or on a night when it was drizzling, he felt lost, lapsed, negative, untended, extinguished, broken and lying down too—unappeasable. And looking up in those kitchenette windows, where the lights were dirty through dirty glass—they *could* wash the windows—was not at all "interesting" to him as it probably was to those guys at the university who had—who had—

Made a football out of Parrington.

Because he knew what it was. He knew it was a mess! He knew it wasn't "colorful," "exotic," "fascinating."

He wanted a dog. A good dog. No mongrel. An apartment—well-furnished, containing a good bookcase, filled with good books in good bindings. He wanted a phonograph, and records. The symphonies. And Yehudi Menuhin. He wanted some good art. These things were not extras. They went to make up a good background. The kind of background those guys had.

12

Maud Martha and New York

THE name "New York" glittered in front of her like the silver in the shops on Michigan Boulevard. It was silver, and it was solid, and it was remote: it was behind glass, it was behind bright glass like the silver in the shops. It was not for her. Yet.

When she was out walking, and with grating iron swish a train whipped by, off, above, its passengers were always, for her comfort, New York-bound. She sat inside with them. She leaned back in the plush. She sped, past farms, through tiny towns, where people slept, kissed, quarreled, ate midnight snacks; unfortunate folk who were not New York-bound and never would be.

Maud Martha loved it when her magazines said "New York," described "good" objects there, wonderful people there, recalled fine talk, the bristling or the creamy or the tactfully shimmering ways of life. They showed pictures of rooms with wood paneling, softly glowing, touched up by the compliment of a spot of auburn here, the low burn of a rare binding there. There were ferns in these rooms, and Chinese boxes; bits of dreamlike crystal; a taste of leather. In the advertisement pages, you saw where you could buy six Italian plates for eleven hundred dollars—and you must hurry, for there was just the one set; you saw where you could buy antique French bisque figurines (pale blue and gold) for—for— Her whole body become a hunger, she would pore over these pages. The clothes interested her, too; especially did she care for the pictures of women wearing carelessly, as if they were rags, dresses that were plain but whose prices were not. And the foolish food (her mother's description) enjoyed by New Yorkers fascinated her. They paid ten dollars for an eight-ounce jar of Russian caviar; they ate things called anchovies, and capers; they ate little diamond-shaped cheeses that paprika had but breathed on; they ate bitter-almond macaroons; they ate papaya packed in rum and syrup; they ate peculiar sauces, were free with honey, were lavish with butter, wine and cream.

She bought the New York papers downtown, read of the concerts and plays, studied the book reviews, was intent over the announcements of auctions. She liked the sound of "Fifth Avenue," "Town Hall," "B. Altman," "Hammacher Schlemmer." She was on Fifth Avenue whenever she wanted to be, and she it was who rolled up, silky or furry, in the taxi, was assisted out, and stood, her next step nebulous, before the theaters of the thousand lights, before velvet-lined impossible shops; she it was.

New York, for Maud Martha, was a symbol. Her

idea of it stood for what she felt life ought to be. Jeweled. Polished. Smiling. Poised. Calmly rushing! Straight up and down, yet graceful enough.

She thought of them drinking their coffee there —or tea, as in England. It was afternoon. Lustrous people glided over perfect floors, correctly smiling. They stopped before a drum table, covered with heavy white—and bearing a silver coffee service, old (in the better sense) china, a platter of orange and cinnamon cakes (or was it nutmeg the cakes would have in them?), sugar and cream, a Chinese box, one tall and slender flower. Their host or hostess poured, smiling too, nodding quickly to this one and that one, inquiring gently whether it should be sugar, or cream, or both, or neither. (She was teaching herself to drink coffee with neither.) All was *very* gentle. The voices, no matter how they rose, or even sharpened, had fur at the base. The steps never bragged, or grated in any way on any ear—not that they could very well, on so good a Persian rug, or deep soft carpeting. And the drum table stood in front of a screen, a Japanese one, perhaps, with rich and mellow, bread-textured colors. The people drank and nibbled, while they discussed the issues of the day, sorting, rejecting, revising. Then they went home, quietly, elegantly. They retired to homes not one whit less solid or embroidered than the home of their host or hostess.

What she wanted to dream, and dreamed, was her affair. It pleased her to dwell upon color and soft bready textures and light, on a complex beauty, on gemlike surfaces. What was the matter with that? Besides, who could safely swear that she would never be able to make her dream come true for herself? Not altogether, then!—but slightly?—in some part?

She was eighteen years old, and the world waited. To caress her.

13

low yellow

I KNOW what he is thinking, thought Maud Martha, as she sat on the porch in the porch swing with Paul Phillips. He is thinking that I am all right. That I am really all right. That I will do.

And I am glad of that, because my whole body is singing beside him. And when you feel like that beside a man you ought to be married to him.

I am what he would call—sweet.

But I am certainly not what he would call pretty. Even with all this hair (which I have just assured him, in response to his question, is not "natural," is not good grade or anything like good grade) even with whatever I have that puts a dimple in his heart, even with these nice ears, I am still, definitely, not what he can call pretty if he remains true to what his idea of pretty has always been. Pretty would be a little cream-colored thing with curly hair. Or at the very lowest pretty would be a little curly-haired thing the color of cocoa with a lot of milk in it. Whereas, I am the color of cocoa straight, if you can be even that "kind" to me.

He wonders, as we walk in the street, about the thoughts of the people who look at us. Are they thinking that he could do no better than—me? Then he thinks, Well, hmp! Well, huh!—all the little good-lookin' dolls that have wanted *him*—all the little sweet high-yellows that have ambled slowly past *his* front door—What he would like to tell those secretly snickering ones!—That any day out of the week he can do better than this black gal.

And by my own admission my hair is absolutely knappy.

"Fatherhood," said Paul, "is not exactly in my line. But it would be all right to have a couple or so of kids, good-looking, in my pocket, so to speak."

"I am not a pretty woman," said Maud Martha. "If you married a pretty woman, you could be the father of pretty children. Envied by people. The father of beautiful children."

"But I don't know," said Paul. "Because my features aren't fine. They aren't regular. They're heavy. They're real Negro features. I'm light, or at least I can claim to be a sort of low-toned yellow, and my hair has a teeny crimp. But even so I'm not handsome."

No, there would be little "beauty" getting born out of such a union.

Still, mused Maud Martha, I am what he would call—sweet, and I am good, and he will marry me. Although, he will be thinking, that's what he always says about letting yourself get interested in these incorruptible virgins, that so often your manıood will not let you concede defeat, and before ʼou know it, you have let them steal you, put an nd, perhaps, to your career.

He will fight, of course. He will decide that he ıust think a long time before he lets that happen ıere.

But in the end I'll hook him, even while he's vondering how this marriage will cramp him or ·inch at him—at him, admirer of the gay life, piffy clothes, beautiful yellow girls, natural hair, mooth cars, jewels, night clubs, cocktail lounges, lass.

14

everybody will be surprise

"OF course," said Paul, "we'll have to start smal But it won't be very long before everybody will b surprised."

Maud Martha smiled.

"Your apartment, eventually, will be a drear The *Defender* will come and photograph it." Pau grinned when he said that, but quite literally h believed it. Since he had decided to go ahead an marry her, he meant to "do it up right." Peopl were going to look at his marriage and see onl hings to want. He was going to have a swanky lat. He and Maudie were going to dress well. They vould entertain a lot.

"Listen," said Paul eagerly, "at a store on Forty-hird and Cottage they're selling four rooms of urniture for eighty-nine dollars."

Maud Martha's heart sank.

"We'll go look at it tomorrow," added Paul.

"Paul—do you think we'll have a hard time find-ng a nice place—when the time comes?"

"No. I don't think so. But look here. I think we ught to plan on a stove-heated flat. We could get ne of those cheap."

"Oh, I wouldn't like that. I've always lived in team."

"I've always lived in stove—till a year ago. It's ust as warm. And about fifteen dollars cheaper."

"Then what made your folks move to steam, hen?"

"Ma wanted to live on a better-looking street. ut we can't think about foolishness like that, vhen we're just starting out. Our flat will be hot stuff; the important thing is the flat, not the street we can't study about foolishness like that; but our flat will be hot stuff. We'll have a swell flat."

"When you have stove heat, you have to have those ugly old fat black pipes stretching out all over the room."

"You don't just have to have long ones."

"I don't want any ones."

"You can have a little short one. And the new heaters they got look like radios. You'll like 'em."

Maud Martha silently decided she wouldn't and resolved to hold out firmly against stove heated flats. No stove-heated flats. And no basements. You got T.B. in basements.

"If you think a basement would be better—" began Paul.

"I don't," she interrupted.

"Basements are cheap too."

Was her attitude unco-operative? Should she be wanting to sacrifice more, for the sake of her man A procession of pioneer women strode down her imagination; strong women, bold; praiseworthy faithful, stout-minded; with a stout light beating in the eyes. Women who could stand low temperatures. Women who would toil eminently, to improve the lot of their men. Women who cooked. She thought of herself, dying for her man. It was a beautiful thought.

15

the kitchenette

THEIR home was on the third floor of a great gray stone building. The two rooms were small. The bedroom was furnished with a bed and dresser, old-fashioned, but in fair condition, and a faded occasional chair. In the kitchen were an oilcloth-covered table, two kitchen chairs, one folding chair, a cabinet base, a brown wooden icebox, and a three-burner gas stove. Only one of the burners worked, the housekeeper told them. The janitor would fix the others before they moved in. Maud Martha said she could fix them herself.

"Nope," objected Paul. "The janitor'll do it. That's what they pay him for." There was a bathroom at the end of the hall, which they would have to share with four other families who lived on the floor.

The housekeeper at the kitchenette place did not require a reference. . . .

The *Defender* would never come here with cameras.

Still, Maud Martha was, at first, enthusiastic. She made plans for this home. She would have the janitor move the bed and dresser out, tell Paul to buy a studio couch, a desk chest, a screen, a novelty chair, a white Venetian blind for the first room, and a green one for the kitchen, since the wallpaper there was green (with little red fishes swimming about). Perhaps they could even get a rug. A green one. And green drapes for the windows. Why, this *might* even turn out to be their dream apartment. It was small, but wonders could be wrought here. They could open up an account at L. Fish Furniture Store, pay a little every month. In that way, they could have the essentials right away. Later, they could get a Frigidaire. A baby's bed, when one became necessary, could go behind the screen, and they would have a pure living room.

Paul, after two or three weeks, told her sheepishly that kitchenettes were not so bad. Theirs seemed "cute and cozy" enough, he declared, and for his part, he went on, he was ready to "camp right down" until the time came to "build." Sadly, however, by that time Maud Martha had lost interest in the place, because the janitor had said that the Owner would not allow the furniture to be disturbed. Tenants moved too often. It was not worth the Owner's financial while to make changes, or to allow tenants to make them. They would have to be satisfied with "the apartment" as it was.

Then, one month after their installation, the first roach arrived. Ugly, shiny, slimy, slick-moving.

She had rather see a rat—well, she had rather see a mouse. She had never yet been able to kill a roach. She could not bear to touch one, with foot or stick or twisted paper. She could only stand helpless, frozen, and watch the slick movement suddenly appear and slither, looking doubly evil, across the mirror, before which she had been calmly brushing her hair. And why? Why was he here? For she was scrubbing with water containing melted American Family soap and Lysol every other day.

And these things—roaches, and having to be satisfied with the place as it was—were not the only annoyances that had to be reckoned with. She was becoming aware of an oddness in color and sound and smell about her, the color and sound and smell of the kitchenette building. The color was gray, and the smell and sound had taken on a suggestion of the properties of color, and impressed one as gray, too. The sobbings, the frustrations, the small hates, the large and ugly hates, the little pushing-through love, the boredom, that came to her from behind those walls (some of them beaver-board) via speech and scream and sigh—all these were gray. And the smells of various types of sweat, and of bathing and bodily functions (the bathroom was always in use, someone was always in the bathroom) and of fresh or stale love-making, which rushed in thick fumes to your nostrils as you walked down the hall, or down the stairs—these were *gray*.

There was a whole lot of grayness here.

16

the young couple at home

PAUL had slept through most of the musicale. Three quarters of the time his head had been a heavy knot on her shoulder. At each of her attempts to remove it, he had waked up so suddenly, and had given her a look of such childlike fierceness, that she could only smile.

Now on the streetcar, however—the car was in the garage—he was not sleepy, and he kept "amusing" Maud Martha with little "tricks," such as cocking his head archly and winking at her, or digging her slyly in the ribs, or lifting her hand to his lips, and blowing on it softly, or poking a finger under her chin and raising it awkwardly, or feeling her muscle, then putting her hand on his muscle, so that she could tell the difference. Such as that. "Clowning," he called it. And because he felt that he was making her happy, she tried not to see the uncareful stares and smirks of the other passengers—uncareful and insultingly consolatory. He sat playfully upon part of her thigh. He gently kicked her toe.

Once home, he went immediately to the bathroom. He did not try to mask his need, he was obvious and direct about it.

"He could make," she thought, "a comment or two on what went on at the musicale. Or some little joke. It isn't that I'm unreasonable or stupid. But everything can be done with a little grace. I'm sure of it."

When he came back, he yawned, stretched, smeared his lips up and down her neck, assured her of his devotion, and sat down on the bed to take off his shoes. She picked up *Of Human Bondage,* and sat at the other end of the bed.

"Snuggle up," he invited.

"I thought I'd read awhile."

"I guess I'll read awhile, too," he decided, when his shoes were off and had been kicked into the kitchen. She got up, went to the shoes, put them in the closet. He grinned at her merrily. She was conscious of the grin, but refused to look at him. She went back to her book. He settled down to his. His was a paper-backed copy of *Sex in the Married Life*.

There he sat, slouched down, terribly absorbed, happy in his sock feet, curling his toes inside the socks.

"I want you to read this book," he said, "—but at the right times: one chapter each night before retiring." He reached over, pinched her on the buttock.

She stood again. "Shall I make some cocoa?" she asked pleasantly. "And toast some sandwiches?"

"Say, I'd like that," he said, glancing up briefly.

She toasted rye strips spread with pimento cheese and grated onion. She made cocoa.

They ate, drank, and read together. She read *Of Human Bondage*. He read *Sex in the Married Life*. They were silent.

Five minutes passed. She looked at him. He was asleep. His head had fallen back, his mouth was open—it was a good thing there were no flies—his ankles were crossed. And the feet!—pointing confidently out (no one would harm them). *Sex in the Married Life* was about to slip to the floor. She did not stretch out a hand to save it.

Once she had taken him to a library. While occupied with the card cases she had glanced up, had observed that he, too, was busy among the cards. "Do you want a book?" "No-o. I'm just curious about something. I wondered if there could be a man in the world named Bastard. Sure enough, there is."

Paul's book fell, making a little clatter. But he did not wake up, and she did not get up.

17

Maud Martha spares the mouse

THERE. She had it at last. The weeks it had devoted to eluding her, the tricks, the clever hide-and-go-seeks, the routes it had in all sobriety devised, together with the delicious moments it had, undoubtedly, laughed up its sleeve—all to no ultimate avail. She had that mouse.

It shook its little self, as best it could, in the trap. Its bright black eyes contained no appeal—the little creature seemed to understand that there was no hope of mercy from the eternal enemy, no hope of reprieve or postponement—but a fine small dignity. It waited. It looked at Maud Martha.

She wondered what else it was thinking. Perhaps that there was not enough food in its larder. Perhaps that little Betty, a puny child from the start, would not, now, be getting fed. Perhaps that, now, the family's seasonal house-cleaning, for lack of expert direction, would be left undone. It might be regretting that young Bobby's education was now at an end. It might be nursing personal regrets. No more the mysterious shadows of the kitchenette, the uncharted twists, the unguessed halls. No more the sweet delights of the chase, the charms of being unsuccessfully hounded, thrown at.

Maud Martha could not bear the little look.

"Go home to your children," she urged. "To your wife or husband." She opened the trap. The mouse vanished.

Suddenly, she was conscious of a new cleanness in her. A wide air walked in her. A life had blundered its way into her power and it had been hers to preserve or destroy. She had not destroyed. In the center of that simple restraint was—creation. She had created a piece of life. It was wonderful.

"Why," she thought, as her height doubled, "why, I'm good! I am *good.*"

She ironed her aprons. Her back was straight. Her eyes were mild, and soft with a godlike loving-kindness.

18

we're the only colored people here

WHEN they went out to the car there were just the very finest bits of white powder coming down with an almost comical little ethereal hauteur, to add themselves to the really important, piled-up masses of their kind.

And it wasn't cold.

Maud Martha laughed happily to herself. It was pleasant out, and tonight she and Paul were very close to each other.

He held the door open for her—instead of going

on around to the driving side, getting in, and leaving her to get in at her side as best she might. When he took this way of calling her "lady" and informing her of his love she felt precious, protected, delicious. She gave him an excited look of gratitude. He smiled indulgently.

"Want it to be the Owl again?"

"Oh, no no, Paul. Let's not go there tonight. I feel too good inside for that. Let's go downtown?"

She had to suggest that with a question mark at the end, always. He usually had three protests. Too hard to park. Too much money. Too many white folks. And tonight she could almost certainly expect a no, she feared, because he had come out in his blue work shirt. There was a spot of apricot juice on the collar, too. His shoes were not shined. . . . But he nodded!

"We've never been to the World Playhouse," she said cautiously. "They have a good picture. I'd feel rich in there."

"You really wanta?"

"Please?"

"Sure."

It wasn't like other movie houses. People from the Studebaker Theatre which, as Maud Martha whispered to Paul, was "all-locked-arms" with the World Playhouse, were strolling up and down the lobby, laughing softly, smoking with gentle grace.

"There must be a play going on in there and this is probably an intermission," Maud Martha whispered again.

"I don't know why you feel you got to whisper," whispered Paul. "Nobody else is whispering in here." He looked around, resentfully, wanting to see a few, just a few, colored faces. There were only their own.

Maud Martha laughed a nervous defiant little laugh; and spoke loudly. "There certainly isn't any reason to whisper. Silly, huh."

The strolling women were cleverly gowned. Some of them had flowers or flashers in their hair. They looked—cooked. Well cared-for. And as though they had never seen a roach or a rat in their lives. Or gone without heat for a week. And the men had even edges. They were men, Maud Martha thought, who wouldn't stoop to fret over less than a thousand dollars.

"We're the only colored people here," said Paul.

She hated him a little. "Oh, hell. Who in hell cares."

"Well, what I want to know is, where do you pay the damn fares."

"There's the box office. Go on up."

He went on up. It was closed.

"Well," sighed Maud Martha, "I guess the picture has started already. But we can't have missed much. Go on up to that girl at the candy counter and ask her where we should pay our money."

He didn't want to do that. The girl was lovely and blonde and cold-eyed, and her arms were akimbo, and the set of her head was eloquent. No one else was at the counter.

"Well. We'll wait a minute. And see—"

Maud Martha hated him again. Coward. She ought to flounce over to the girl herself—show him up. . . .

The people in the lobby tried to avoid looking curiously at two shy Negroes wanting desperately not to seem shy. The white women looked at the Negro woman in her outfit with which no special fault could be found, but which made them think, somehow, of close rooms, and wee, close lives. They looked at her hair. They liked to see a dark colored girl with long, long hair. They were always slightly surprised, but agreeably so, when they did. They supposed it was the hair that had got her that yellowish, good-looking Negro man.

The white men tried not to look at the Negro man in the blue work shirt, the Negro man without a tie.

An usher opened a door of the World Playhouse part and ran quickly down the few steps that led from it to the lobby. Paul opened his mouth.

"Say, fella. Where do we get the tickets for the movie?"

The usher glanced at Paul's feet before answering. Then he said coolly, but not unpleasantly, "I'll take the money."

They were able to go in.

And the picture! Maud Martha was so glad that they had not gone to the Owl! Here was technicolor, and the love story was sweet. And there was classical music that silvered its way into you and made your back cold. And the theater itself! It was no palace, no such Great Shakes as the Tivoli out south, for instance (where many colored people went every night). But you felt good sitting there, yes, good, and as if, when you left it, you would be going home to a sweet-smelling apartment with flowers on little gleaming tables; and wonderful silver on night-blue velvet, in chests; and crackly sheets; and lace spreads on such beds as you saw at Marshall Field's. Instead of back to your kit'n't apt., with the garbage of your floor's families in a big can just outside your door, and the gray sound of little gray feet scratching away from it as you drag up those flights of narrow complaining stairs.

Paul pressed her hand. Paul said, "We oughta do this more often."

And again. "We'll have to do this more often. And go to plays, too. I mean at that Blackstone, and Studebaker."

She pressed back, smiling beautifully to herself in the darkness. Though she knew that once the spell was over it would be a year, two years, more, before he would return to the World Playhouse. And he might never go to a real play. But she was learning to love moments. To love moments for themselves.

When the picture was over, and the lights revealed them for what they were, the Negroes stood up among the furs and good cloth and faint perfume, looked about them eagerly. They hoped they would meet no cruel eyes. They hoped no one would look intruded upon. They had enjoyed the picture so, they were so happy, they wanted to laugh, to say warmly to the other outgoers, "Good, huh? Wasn't it swell?"

This, of course, they could not do. But if only no one would look intruded upon. . . .

19

if you're light and have long hair

CAME the invitation that Paul recognized as an honor of the first water, and as sufficient indication that he was, at last, a social somebody. The invitation was from the Foxy Cats Club, the club of clubs. He was to be present, in formal dress, at the Annual Foxy Cats Dawn Ball. No chances were taken: "Top hat, white tie and tails" hastily followed the "Formal dress," and that elucidation was in bold type.

Twenty men were in the Foxy Cats Club. All were good-looking. All wore clothes that were rich and suave. All "handled money," for their number consisted of well-located barbers, policemen, "government men" and men with a lucky touch at the tracks. Certainly the Foxy Cats Club was not a representative of that growing group of South Side organizations devoted to moral and civic improvements, or to literary or other cultural pursuits. If that had been so, Paul would have chucked his bid (which was black and silver, decorated with winking cat faces) down the toilet with a yawn. "That kind of stuff" was hardly understood by Paul, and was always dismissed with an airy "dicty," "hincty" or "high-falutin'." But no. The Foxy Cats devoted themselves solely to the business of being "hep," and each year they spent hundreds of dollars on their wonderful Dawn Ball, which did not begin at dawn, but was scheduled to end at dawn. "Ball," they called the frolic, but it served also the purposes of party, feast and fashion show. Maud Martha, watching him study his invitation, watching him lift his chin, could see that he considered himself one of the blessed.

Who—what kind soul had recommended him!

"He'll have to take me," thought Maud Martha. "For the envelope is addressed 'Mr. and Mrs.,' and I opened it. I guess he'd like to leave me home. At the Ball, there will be only beautiful girls, or real stylish ones. There won't be more than a handful like me. My type is not a Foxy Cat favorite. But he can't avoid taking me—since he hasn't yet thought of words or ways strong enough, and at the same time soft enough—for he's kind: he doesn't like to injure—to carry across to me the news that he is not to be held permanently by my type, and that he can go on with this marriage only if I put no ropes or questions around him. Also, he'll want to humor me, now that I'm pregnant."

She would need a good dress. That, she knew, could be a problem, on his grocery clerk's pay. He would have his own expenses. He would have to rent his topper and tails, and he would have to buy a fine tie, and really excellent shoes. She knew he was thinking that on the strength of his appearance and sophisticated behavior at this Ball might depend his future admission (for why not dream?) to *membership,* actually, in the Foxy Cats Club!

"I'll settle," decided Maud Martha, "on a plain white princess-style thing and some blue and black satin ribbon. I'll go to my mother's. I'll work miracles at the sewing machine.

"On that night, I'll wave my hair. I'll smell faintly of lily of the valley."

The main room of the Club 99, where the Ball was held, was hung with green and yellow and red balloons, and the thick pillars, painted to give an effect of marble, and stretching from floor to ceiling, were draped with green and red and yellow crepe paper. Huge ferns, rubber plants and bowls of flowers were at every corner. The floor itself was a decoration, golden, glazed. There was no overhead light; only wall lamps, and the bulbs in these were romantically dim. At the back of the room, standing on a furry white rug, was the long banquet table, dressed in damask, accented by groups of thin silver candlesticks bearing white candles, and laden with lovely food: cold chicken, lobster, candied ham fruit combinations, potato salad in a great gold dish, corn sticks, a cheese fluff in spiked tomato cups, fruit cake, angel cake, sunshine cake. The drinks were at a smaller table nearby, behind which stood a genial mixologist, quick with maraschino cherries, and with lemon, ice and liquor. Wines were there, and whiskey, and rum, and eggnog made with pure cream.

Paul and Maud Martha arrived rather late, on purpose. Rid of their wraps, they approached the glittering floor. Bunny Bates's orchestra was playing Ellington's "Solitude."

Paul, royal in rented finery, was flushed with excitement. Maud Martha looked at him. Not very tall. Not very handsomely made. But there was that extraordinary quality of maleness. Hiding in the body that was not *too* yellow, waiting to spring out at her, surround her (she liked to think) —that maleness. The Ball stirred her. The Beauties, in their gorgeous gowns, bustling, supercilious; the young men, who at other times most unpleasantly blew their noses, and darted surreptitiously into alleys to relieve themselves, and sweated and swore at their jobs, and scratched their more intimate parts, now smiling, smooth, overgallant; the drowsy lights; the smells of food and flowers, the smell of Murray's pomade, the body perfumes, natural and superimposed; the sensuous heaviness of the wine-colored draperies at the many windows; the music, now steamy and slow, now as clear and fragile as glass, now raging, passionate, now moaning and thickly gray. The Ball made toys of her emotions, stirred her variously. But she was anxious to have it end, she was anxious to be at home again, with the door closed behind herself and her husband. Then, he might be warm. There might be more than the absent courtesy he had been giving her of late. Then, he might be the tree she had a great need to lean against, in this "emergency." There was no telling what dear thing he might say to her, what little gem let fall.

But, to tell the truth, his behavior now was not very promising of gems to come. After their second dance he escorted her to a bench by the wall, left her. Trying to look nonchalant, she sat. She sat, trying not to show the inferiority she did not feel. When the music struck up again, he began to dance with someone red-haired and curved, and white as a white. Who was she? He had approached her easily, he had taken her confidently, he held her and conversed with her as though he had known her well for a long, long time. The girl smiled up at him. Her gold-spangled bosom was pressed—was pressed against that maleness—

A man asked Maud Martha to dance. He was dark, too. His mustache was small.

"Is this your first Foxy Cats?" he asked.

"What?" Paul's cheek was on that of Gold-Spangles.

"First Cats?"

"Oh. Yes." Paul and Gold-Spangles were weaving through the noisy twisting couples, were trying, apparently, to get to the reception hall.

"Do you know that girl? What's her name?" Maud Martha asked her partner, pointing to Gold-Spangles. Her partner looked, nodded. He pressed her closer.

"That's Maella. That's Maella."

"Pretty, isn't she?" She wanted him to keep talking about Maella. He nodded again.

"Yep. She has 'em howling along the stroll, all right, all right."

Another man, dancing past with an artificial redhead, threw a whispered word at Maud Martha's partner, who caught it eagerly, winked. "Solid, ol' man," he said. "Solid, Jack." He pressed Maud Martha closer. "You're a babe," he said. "You're a real babe." He reeked excitingly of tobacco, liquor, pinesoap, toilet water, and Sen Sen.

Maud Martha thought of her parents' back yard. Fresh. Clean. Smokeless. In her childhood, a snowball bush had shone there, big above the dandelions. The snowballs had been big, healthy. Once, she and her sister and brother had waited in the back yard for their parents to finish readying themselves for a trip to Milwaukee. The snowballs had been so beautiful, so fat and startlingly white in the sunlight, that she had suddenly loved home a thousand times more than ever before, and had not wanted to go to Milwaukee. But as the children grew, the bush sickened. Each year the snowballs were smaller and more dispirited. Finally a summer came when there were no blossoms at all. Maud Martha wondered what had become of the bush. For it was not there now. Yet she, at least, had never seen it go.

"Not," thought Maud Martha, "that they love each other. It oughta be that simple. Then I could lick it. It oughta be that easy. But it's my color that makes him mad. I try to shut my eyes to that, but it's no good. What I am inside, what is really me, he likes okay. But he keeps looking at my color, which is like a wall. He has to jump over it in order to meet and touch what I've got for him. He has to jump away up high in order to see it. He gets awful tired of all that jumping."

Paul came back from the reception hall. Maella was clinging to his arm. A final cry of the saxophone finished that particular slice of the blues. Maud Martha's partner bowed, escorted her to a chair by a rubber plant, bowed again, left.

"I could," considered Maud Martha, "go over there and scratch her upsweep down. I could spit on her back. I could scream. 'Listen,' I could scream, 'I'm making a baby for this man and I mean to do it in peace.' "

But if the root was sour what business did she have up there hacking at a leaf?

20

a birth

AFTER dinner, they washed dishes together. Then they undressed, and Paul got in bed, and was asleep almost instantly. She went down the long public hall to the bathroom, in her blue chenille robe. On her way back down the squeezing dark of the hall she felt—something softly separate in her. Back in the bedroom, she put on her gown, then stepped to the dresser to smear her face with cold cream. But when she turned around to get in the bed she couldn't move. Her legs cramped painfully, and she had a tremendous desire to eliminate which somehow she felt she would never be able to gratify.

"Paul!" she cried. As though in his dreams he had been waiting to hear that call, and that call only, he was up with a bound.

"I can't move."

He rubbed his eyes.

"Maudie, are you kidding?"

"I'm not kidding, Paul. I can't move."

He lifted her up and laid her on the bed, his eyes stricken.

"Look here, Maudie. Do you think you're going to have that baby tonight?"

"No—no. These are just what they call 'false pains.' I'm not going to have the baby tonight. Can you get—my gown off?"

"Sure. Sure."

But really he was afraid to touch her. She lay nude on the bed for a few moments, perfectly still. Then all of a sudden motion came to her. Whereas before she had not been able to move her legs, now she could not keep them still.

"Oh, my God," she prayed aloud. "Just let my legs get still five minutes." God did not answer the prayer.

Paul was pacing up and down the room in fright.

"Look here. I don't think those are false pains. I think you're going to have that baby tonight."

"Don't say that, Paul," she muttered between clenched teeth. "I'm not going to have the baby tonight."

"I'm going to call your mother."

"Don't do that, Paul. She can't stand to see things like this. Once she got a chance to see a still-born baby, but she fainted before they even unwrapped it. She can't stand to see things like this. False pains, that's all. Oh, God, why don't you let me keep my legs still!"

She began to whimper in a manner that made Paul want to vomit. His thoughts traveled to the girl he had met at the Dawn Ball several months before. Cool. Sweet. Well-groomed. Fair.

"You're going to have that baby *now.* I'm going down to call up your mother and a doctor."

"DON'T YOU GO OUT OF HERE AND LEAVE ME ALONE! Damn. DAMN!"

"All right. All right. I won't leave you alone. I'll get the woman next door to come in. But somebody's got to get a doctor here."

"Don't you sneak out! Don't you *sneak* out!" She was pushing down with her stomach now. Paul, standing at the foot of the bed with his hands in his pockets, saw the creeping insistence of what he thought was the head of the child.

"Oh, my Lord!" he cried. "It's coming! It's coming!"

He walked about the room several times. He went to the dresser and began to brush his hair. She looked at him in speechless contempt. He went out of the door, and ran down the three flights of stairs two or three steps at a time. The telephone was on the first floor. No sooner had he picked up the receiver than he heard Maud Martha give what he was sure could *only* be called a "bloodcurdling scream." He bolted up the stairs, saw her wriggling on the bed, said softly, "Be right back," and bolted down again. First he called his mother's doctor, and begged him to come right over. Then he called the Browns.

"Get her to the hospital!" shouted Belva Brown. "You'll have to get her to the hospital right away!"

"I can't. She's having the baby now. She isn't going to let anybody touch her. I tell you, she's having the baby."

"Don't be a fool. Of course she can get to the hospital. Why, she mustn't have it there in the house! I'm coming over there. I'll take her myself. Be sure there's plenty of gas in that car."

He tried to reach his mother. She was out—had not returned from a revival meeting.

When Paul ran back up the stairs, he found young Mrs. Cray, who lived in the front apartment of their floor, attending his shrieking wife.

"I heard 'er yellin', and thought I'd better come

in, seein' as how you all is so confused. Got a doctor comin'?"

Paul sighed heavily. "I just called one. Thanks for coming in. This—this came on all of a sudden, and I don't think I know what to do."

"Well, the thing to do is get a doctor right off. She's goin' to have the baby soon. Call *my* doctor." She gave him a number. "Whichever one gets here first can work on her. Ain't no time to waste."

Paul ran back down the stairs and called the number. "What's the doctor's address?" he yelled up. Mrs. Cray yelled it down. He went out to get the doctor personally. He was glad of an excuse to escape. He was sick of hearing Maudie scream. He had had no idea that she could scream that kind of screaming. It was awful. How lucky he was that he had been born a man. How lucky he was that he had been born a man!

Belva arrived in twenty minutes. She was grateful to find another woman present. She had come to force Maud Martha to start for the hospital, but a swift glance told her that the girl would not leave her bed for many days. As she said to her husband and Helen later on, "The baby was all ready to spill out."

When her mother came in the door Maud Martha tightened her lips, temporarily forgetful of her strange pain. (But it wasn't pain. It was something else.) "Listen. If you're going to make a fuss, go on out. I'm having enough trouble without you making a fuss over everything."

Mrs. Cray giggled encouragingly. Belva said bravely, "I'm not going to make a fuss. You'll see. Why, there's nothing to make a fuss *about*. You're just going to have a baby, like millions of other women. Why should I make a fuss?"

Maud Martha tried to smile but could not quite make it. The sensations were getting grindingly sharp. She screamed longer and louder, explaining breathlessly in between times, "I just can't help it. Excuse me."

"Why, go on and scream," urged Belva. "You're supposed to scream. That's your privilege. I'm sure *I* don't mind." Her ears were splitting, and over and over as she stood there looking down at her agonized daughter, she said to herself, "Why doesn't the doctor come? Why doesn't the doctor come? I know I'm going to faint." She and Mrs. Cray stood, one on each side of the bed, purposelessly holding a sheet over Maud Martha, under which they peeped as seldom as they felt was safe. Maud Martha kept asking, "Has the head come?" Presently she felt as though her whole body were having a bowel movement. The head came. Then, with a little difficulty, the wide shoulders. Then easily, with soft and slippery smoothness, out slipped the rest of the body and the baby was born. The first thing it did was sneeze.

Maud Martha laughed as though she could never bear to stop. "Listen to him sneeze. My little baby. Don't let him drown, Mrs. Cray." Mrs. Cray looked at Maud Martha, because she did not want to look at the baby. "How you know it's a him?" Maud Martha laughed again.

Belva also refused to look at the baby. "See, Maudie," she said, "see how brave I was? The baby is born, and I didn't get nervous or faint or anything. Didn't I tell you?"

"Now isn't that nice," thought Maud Martha. "Here I've had the baby, and she thinks I should praise her for having stood up there and looked on." Was it, she suddenly wondered, as hard to watch suffering as it was to bear it?

Five minutes after the birth, Paul got back with Mrs. Cray's doctor, a large silent man, who came in swiftly, threw the sheet aside without saying a word, cut the cord. Paul looked at the new human being. It appeared gray and greasy. Life was hard, he thought. What had he done to deserve a stillborn child? But there it was, lying dead.

"It's dead, isn't it?" he asked dully.

"Oh, get out of here!" cried Mrs. Cray, pushing him into the kitchen and shutting the door.

"Girl," said the doctor. Then grudgingly, "Fine girl."

"Did you hear what the doctor said, Maudie?" chattered Belva. "You've got a daughter, the doctor says." The doctor looked at her quickly.

"Say, you'd better go out and take a walk around the block. You don't look so well."

Gratefully, Belva obeyed. When she got back, Mrs. Cray and the doctor had oiled and dressed the baby—dressed her in an outfit found in Maud Martha's top dresser drawer. Belva looked at the newcomer in amazement.

"Well, she's a little beauty, isn't she!" she cried. She had not expected a handsome child.

Maud Martha's thoughts did not dwell long on the fact of the baby. There would be all her life long for that. She preferred to think, now, about how well she felt. Had she ever in her life felt so well? She felt well enough to get up. She folded her arms triumphantly across her chest, as another young woman, her neighbor to the rear, came in.

"Hello, Mrs. Barksdale!" she hailed. "Did you hear the news? I just had a baby, and I feel strong enough to go out and shovel coal! Having a baby is *nothing,* Mrs. Barksdale. Nothing at all."

"Aw, yeah?" Mrs. Barksdale smacked her gum admiringly. "Well, from what I heard back there a while ago, didn't seem like it was nothing. Girl, I didn't know anybody *could* scream that loud." Maud Martha tittered. Oh, she felt fine. She wondered why Mrs. Barksdale hadn't come in while the screaming was going on; she had missed it all.

People. Weren't they sweet. She had never said more than "Hello, Mrs. Barksdale" and "Hello, Mrs. Cray" to these women before. But as soon as something happened to her, in they trooped. People were sweet.

The doctor brought the baby and laid it in the bed beside Maud Martha. Shortly before she had heard it in the kitchen—a bright delight had flooded through her upon first hearing that part of Maud Martha Brown Phillips expressing itself with a voice of its own. But now the baby was quiet and returned its mother's stare with one that seemed equally curious and mystified but perfectly cool and undisturbed.

21

posts

PEOPLE have to choose something decently constant to depend on, thought Maud Martha. People must have something to lean on.

But the love of a single person was not enough. Not only was personal love itself, however good, a thing that varied from week to week, from second to second, but the parties to it were likely, for example, to die, any minute, or otherwise be parted, or destroyed. At any time.

Not alone was the romantic love of a man and a

woman fallible, but the breadier love between parents and children; brothers; animals; friend and friend. Those too could not be heavily depended on.

Could be nature, which had a seed, or root, or an element (what do you want to call it) of constancy, under all that system of change. Of course, to say "system" at all implied arrangement, and therefore some order of constancy.

Could be, she mused, a marriage. The marriage shell, not the romance, or love, it might contain. A marriage, the plainer, the more plateaulike, the better. A marriage made up of Sunday papers and shoeless feet, baking powder biscuits, baby baths, and matinees and laundrymen, and potato plants in the kitchen window.

Was, perhaps, the whole life of man a dedication to this search for something to lean upon, and was, to a great degree, his "happiness" or "unhappiness" written up for him by the demands or limitations of what he chose for that work?

For work it was. Leaning was a work.

22

tradition and Maud Martha

WHAT she had wanted was a solid. She had wanted shimmering form; warm, but hard as stone and as difficult to break. She had wanted to found—tradition. She had wanted to shape, for their use, for hers, for his, for little Paulette's, a set of falterless customs. She had wanted stone: here she was, being wife to *him*, salving him, in every way considering and replenishing him—in short, here she was celebrating Christmas night by passing pretzels and beer.

He had done his part, was his claim. He had, had he not? lugged in a Christmas tree. So he had waited till early Christmas morning, when a tree was cheap; so he could not get the lights to burn; so the tinsel was insufficient and the gold balls few. He had promised a tree and he had gotten a tree, and that should be enough for everybody. Furthermore, Paulette had her blocks, her picture book, her doll buggy and her doll. So the doll's left elbow was chipped: more than that would be chipped before Paulette was through! And if the doll buggy was not like the Gold Coast buggies, that was too bad; that was too, too bad for Maud Martha, for Paulette. Here he was, whipping himself to death daily, that Maud Martha's stomach and Paulette's stomach might receive bread and milk and navy beans with tomato catsup, and he was taken to task because he had not furnished, in addition, a velvet-lined buggy with white-walled wheels! Oh yes that *was* what Maud Martha wanted, for her precious princess daughter, and no use denying. But she could just get out and work, that was all. She could just get out and grab herself a job and buy some of these beans and buggies. And in the meantime, she could just help entertain his friends. She was his wife, and he was the head of the family, and on Christmas night the least he could do, by God, and *would* do, by God, was stand his friends a good mug of beer. And to heck with, in fact, to hell with, her fruitcakes and coffees. Put Paulette to bed.

At Home, the buying of the Christmas tree was a ritual. Always it had come into the Brown household four days before Christmas, tall, but not too tall, and not too wide. Tinsel, bulbs, little Santa Clauses and snowmen, and the pretty gold and silver and colored balls did not have to be renewed oftener than once in five years because after Christmas they were always put securely away, on a special shelf in the basement, where they rested for a year. Black walnut candy, in little flat white sheets, crunchy, accompanied the tree, but it was never eaten until Christmas eve. Then, late at night, a family decorating party was held, Maud

Martha, Helen and Harry giggling and teasing and occasionally handing up a ball or Santa Claus, while their father smiled benignly over all and strung and fitted and tinseled, and their mother brought in the black walnut candy and steaming cups of cocoa with whipped cream, and plain shortbread. And everything peaceful, sweet!

And there were the other customs. Easter customs. In childhood, never till Easter morning was "the change" made, the change from winter to spring underwear. Then, no matter how cold it happened to be, off came the heavy trappings and out, for Helen and Maud Martha, were set the new little patent leather shoes and white socks, the little b.v.d.'s and light petticoats, and for Harry, the new brown oxfords, and white shorts and sleeveless undershirts. The Easter eggs had always been dyed the night before, and in the morning, before Sunday school, the Easter baskets, full of chocolate eggs and candy bunnies and cotton bunnies, were handed round, but not eaten from until after Sunday school, and even then not much!—

because there was more candy coming, and dyed eggs, too, to be received (and eaten on the spot) at the Sunday School Children's Easter Program, on which every one of them recited until Maud Martha was twelve.

What of October customs?—of pumpkins yellowly burning; of polished apples in a water-green bowl; of sheets for ghost costumes, surrendered up by Mama with a sigh?

And birthdays, with their pink and white cakes and candles, strawberry ice cream, and presents wrapped up carefully and tied with wide ribbons: whereas here was this man, who never considered giving his own mother a birthday bouquet, and dropped in his wife's lap a birthday box of drugstore candy (when he thought of it) wrapped in the drugstore green.

The dinner table, at home, was spread with a white white cloth, cheap but white and very white, and whatever was their best in china sat in cheerful dignity, firmly arranged, upon it. This man was not a lover of tablecloths, he could eat from a splintery board, he could eat from the earth.

She passed round Blatz, and inhaled the smoke of the guests' cigarettes, and watched the soaked tissue that had enfolded the corner Chicken Inn's burned barbecue drift listlessly to her rug. She removed from her waist the arm of Chuno Jones, Paul's best friend.

23

kitchenette folk

OF the people in her building, Maud Martha wa most amused by Oberto, who had the largest fla of all, a three-roomer on the first floor.

Oberto was a happy man. He had a nice littl going grocery store. He had his health. And, mos important, he had his little lovely wife Marie.

Some folks did not count Marie among his bless ings. She never got up before ten. Oberto mus prepare his breakfast or go breakfastless. As a rule e made only coffee, leaving one cup of it in the ot for her. At ten or after, in beautiful solitude, he would rise, bathe and powder for an hour, hen proceed to the kitchen, where she heated that offee, fried bacon and eggs for herself, and toasted aisin bread.

Marie dusted and swept infrequently, scrubbed nly when the floors were heavy with dirt and rease. Her meals were generally underdone or urned. She sent the laundry out every week, but nore often than not left the clothes (damp) in the ag throughout the week, spilling them out a few ninutes before she expected the laundryman's ext call, that the bag might again be stuffed with lirty clothes and carried off. Oberto's shirts were inished at the laundry. Underwear he wore rough-dried. Her own clothes, however, she ironed with egularity and care.

Such domestic sins were shocking enough. But people accused her of yet more serious crimes. It vas well thought on the south side that Oberto's vife was a woman of affairs, barely taking time to lay one down before she gathered up another. I was rumored, too, but not confirmed, that now an then she was obliged to make quiet calls of busines on a certain Madame Lomiss, of Thirty-fourth an Calumet.

But Oberto was happy. The happiest man, h argued, in his community. True enough, Wilma the wife of Magnicentius, the Thirty-ninth Stree barber, baked rolls of white and fluffy softness. Bu Magnicentius himself could not deny that Wilm was a filthy woman, and wore stockings two days at least, before she washed them. He even made n secret of the fact that she went to bed in ragged dire, cotton nightgowns.

True, too, Viota, the wife of Leon, the Coca Cola truck driver, not only ironed her husband' shirts, but did all the laundry work herself, begin ning early every Monday morning—scrubbing th sheets, quilts, blankets, and slip covers with he own hefty hand. But Leon himself could not deny that Viota was a boisterous, big woman with a voice of wonderful power, and eyes of pink treaked yellow and a nose that never left off niffing.

Who, further, would question the truth that Nathalia, the wife of John the laundryman, kept her house shining, and smelling of Lysol and Gold Dust at all times, and that every single Saturday night she washed down the white walls of her perfect kitchen? But verily who (of an honorable tongue) could deny that the active-armed Nathalia had little or no acquaintance with the deodorant qualities of Mum, Hush, or Quiet?

Remembering Nathalia, and remembering Wilma and Viota, Oberto thanked his lucky stars that he had had sense enough to marry his dainty little Marie, who spoke in modulated tones (almost in a whisper), who wore filmy black nightgowns, who bathed always once and sometimes twice a day in water generously treated with sweet bath crystals, and fluffed herself all over with an expensive lavender talcum, and creamed her arms and legs with a rosy night cream, and powdered her face, that was reddish brown (like an Indian's!)

with a stuff that the movie stars preferred, aı
wore clothes out of *Vogue* and *Harper's Bazaa*
and favored Kleenex, and dressed her hair in
smart upsweep, and pinned silver flowers at h
ears, and used My Sin perfume.

He loved to sit and watch her primp before t
glass.

She didn't know whether she liked a little or
lot (a person could not always tell) the whi
woman married to a West Indian who lived in t
third-floor kitchenette next Maud Martha's ow
Through the day and night this woman, Euge
Banks, sang over and over again—varying t
choruses, using what undoubtedly were her ow
improvisations, for they were very bad—the sa
popular song. Maud Martha had her own ide
about popular songs. "A popular song," thoug
she, "especially if it's one of the old, soft ones,
beautiful, sometimes, and seems to touch yo
mood exactly. But the touch is usually not fu
You rise up with a popular song, but it isn't able t

se as high, once it has you started, as you are; by ne time you've risen as high as it can take you you an't bear to stop, and you swell up and up and up ll you're swelled to bursting. The popular music as long ago given up and left you."

This woman would come over, singing or humming her popular song, to see Maud Martha, anting to know what special technique was to be sed in dealing with a Negro man; a Negro man as a special type man; she knew that there should e, indeed, that there had to be, a special technique to be used with this type man, but what? nd after all, there should be more than—than nging across the sock washing, the cornbread aking, the fish frying. No, she had not expected ealth, no—but he had seemed so exciting! so rimitive!—life with a Negro man had looked, rom the far side, like adventure—and the nights *ere* good; but there were precious few of the ights, because he stayed away for days (though hen he came back he was "very swell" and would ang up a picture or varnish a chair or let her make him some crêpes suzette, which she had al ways made so well).

Her own mother would not write to her; and sh was, Mrs. Eugena Banks whined, beginning t wonder if it had not all been a mistake; could sh not go back to Dayton? could she not begin again

Then there was Clement Lewy, a little boy a the back, on the second floor.

Lewy life was not terrifically tossed. Saltless rather. Or like an unmixed batter. Lumpy.

Little Clement's mother had grown listless afte the desertion. She looked as though she had bee scrubbed, up and down, on the washing board doused from time to time in gray and noisom water. But little Clement looked alert, he looke happy, he was always spirited. He was in secon grade. He did his work, and had always been pro moted. At home he sang. He recited little poems He told his mother little stories wound out of th air by himself. His mother glanced at him once i while. She would have been proud of him if she ad had the time.

She started toward her housemaid's work each norning at seven. She left a glass of milk and a owl of dry cereal and a dish of prunes on the able, and set the alarm clock for eight. At eight ttle Clement punched off the alarm, stretched, ot up, washed, dressed, combed, brushed, ate his reakfast. It was quiet in the apartment. He hurried off to school. At noon he returned from school, pened the door with his key. It was quiet in the partment. He poured himself a second glass of nilk, got more prunes, and ate a slice—"just one lice," his mother had cautioned—of bread and utter. He went back to school. At three o'clock he eturned from school, opened the door with his ey. It was quiet in the apartment. He got a couple f graham crackers out of the cookie can. He drew imself a glass of water. He changed his clothes. Then he went out to play, leaving behind him the wo rooms. Leaving behind him the brass beds, the amp with the faded silk tassel and frayed cord, the hooked oven door, the cracks in the walls and th quiet. As he played, he kept a lookout for h mother, who usually arrived at seven, or near tha hour. When he saw her rounding the corner, h little face underwent a transformation. His ey lashed into brightness, his lips opened suddenl and became a smile, and his eyebrows climbed to ward his hairline in relief and joy.

He would run to his mother and almost thro his little body at her. "Here I am, mother! Here am! Here I am!"

There was, or there had been, Richard—whos weekly earnings as a truck driver for a small bev erage concern had dropped, slyly, from twenty five, twenty-three, twenty-one, to sixteen, fifteen twelve, while his weekly rent remained what it wa (the family of five lived in one of the one-room apartments, a whole dollar cheaper than such two-room as Paul and Maud Martha occupied) his family food and clothing bills had not dropped and altogether it had been too much, the neve

ıving enough to buy Pabst or Ninety Proof for
e boys, the being scared to death to offer a man
couple of cigarettes for fear your little supply,
ıd with it your little weak-kneed nonchalance,
ight be exhausted before the appearance of your
:xt pay envelope (pink, and designated elab-
ately on the outside, "Richard"), the coming
ıck at night, every night, to a billowy diaper
orld, a wife with wild hair, twin brats screaming,
ıd writhing, and wetting their crib, and a third
'at, leaping on, from, and about chairs and table
ith repeated Hi-yo Silvers, and the sitting down
a meal never quite adequate, never quite—de-
ɔite all your sacrifices, your inability to "treat"
ɔur friends, your shabby rags, your heartache.
. . It was altogether too much, so one night he
ad simply failed to come home.

There was an insane youth of twenty, twice re-
:ased from Dunning. He had a smooth tan face,
verlaid with oil. His name was Binnie. Or per-
aps it was Bennie, or Benjamin. But his mother

lovingly called him "Binnie." Binnie strode tl halls, with huge eyes, direct and annoyed. I strode, and played "catch" with a broken watc which was attached to a long string wound arour his left arm. There was no annoyance in his ey when he spoke to Maud Martha, though, ar none in his nice voice. He was very fond of Mau Martha. Once, when she answered a rap c the door, there he was, and he pushed in befo she could open her mouth. He had on a new be he said. "My Uncle John gave it to me," he sai "So my pants won't fall down." He walked abo the apartment, after closing the door with a car ful sneer. He touched things. He pulled a pet from a pink rose with savage anger, then kissed with a tenderness that was more terrible than tl anger; briskly he rapped on the table, turned suc denly to stare at her, to see if she approved c what he was doing—she smiled uncertainly; I saw the big bed, fingered it, sat on it, got u kicked it. He opened a dresser drawer, took out ruler. "This is ni-ice—but I won't take it" (wit rm decision, noble virtue). "I'll put it back." He ɔoke of his aunt, his Uncle John's wife Octavia. She's ni-ice—you know, she can even call me, nd I don't even get mad." With another careful ıeer, he opened the door. He went out.

Mrs. Teenie Thompson. Fifty-three; and pep-er whenever she talked of the North Shore people ʼho had employed her as housemaid for ten years. She went to huggin' and kissin' of me—course I ot to receive it—I got to work for 'em. But they ıink they got me thinkin' they love me. Then I'm ıpposed to kill my silly self slavin' for 'em. To be ʼorthy of their love. These old whi' folks. They ve you, honey. Well, I jive 'em just like they ve me. They can't beat me jivin'. They'll have ɔ jive much, to come anywhere *near* my mark in vin'."

About one of the one-roomers, a little light ʼoman flitted. She was thin and looked ill. Her air, which was long and of a strangely flat blackness, hung absolutely still, no matter how much i mistress moved. If anyone passed her usually ope door, she would nod cheerily, but she rarely spok Chiefly you would see her flitting, in a faded blu rayon housecoat, touching this, picking up tha adjusting, arranging, posing prettily. She was Mr Whitestripe. Mr. Whitestripe was a dark and daj per young man of medium height, with a sma soot-smear of a mustache. The Whitestripes we the happiest couple Maud Martha had ever me They were soft-spoken, kind to each other, we worried about each other. "Now you watch th cough now, Coopie!" For that was what she calle him. "Here, take this Rem, here, take this lemc juice." "You wrap up good, now, you put on th scarf, Coo!" For that was what he called her. C (rushing out of the door in his undershirt, or shoe off) "Did I hear you stumble down ther Coo? Did I hear you hurt your knee?" Ofte visiting them, you were embarrassed, because was obvious that you were interrupting the pro ress of a truly great love; even as you converse here they would be, kissing or patting each other, r gazing into each other' eyes. Most fitting was it hat adjacent to their "domicile" was the balcony f the building. Unfortunately, it was about two ıches wide. Three pressures of a firm foot, and he little balcony would crumble downward to ıingle with other dust. The Whitestripes never at on it, but Maud Martha had no doubt that ften on summer evenings they would open the imsy "French" door, and stand there gazing out, ıinking of what little they knew about Romeo nd Juliet, their arms about each other.

"It is such a beautiful story," sighed Maud Iartha once, to Paul.

"What is?"

"The love story of the Whitestripes."

"Well, I'm no 'Coopie' Whitestripe," Paul had bserved, sharply, "so you can stop mooning. I'll ever be a 'Coopie' Whitestripe."

"No," agreed Maud Martha. "No, you never vill."

The one-roomer next the Whitestripes was occupied by Maryginia Washington, a maiden of sixty-eight, or sixty-nine, or seventy, a becrutched, gnarled, bleached lemon with smartly bobbed white hair; who claimed, and proudly, to be an "indirect" descendant of the first President of the United States; who loathed the darker members of her race but did rather enjoy playing the *grande dame,* a hobbling, denture-clacking version, for their benefit, while they played, at least in her imagination, Topsys—and did rather enjoy advising them, from time to time, to apply lightening creams to the horror of their flesh—"because they ain't no sense in lookin' any worser'n you have to, is they, dearie?"

In the fifth section, on the third floor, lived a Woman of Breeding. Her name was Josephine Snow. She was too much of a Woman of Breeding to allow the title "Madame" to vulgarize her name, but certain inhabitants of the building had all they could do to keep from calling her

"Madame Snow," and eventually they relaxed, and called her that as a matter of course, behind her back.

Madame Snow was the color of soured milk, about sixty, and very superior to her surroundings —although she was not a Maryginia Washington. She had some sort of mysterious income, for although she had lived for seven years in "Gappington Arms" (the name given the building by the tenants, in dubious honor of the autocratic lady owner) no one had ever seen her go out to work. She rarely went anywhere. She went to church no more than once a month, and she sent little Clement Lewy and other children in the building to the store. She maintained a standard rate of pay; no matter how far the errand runner had to go, nor how heavily-loaded he was to be upon his return, she paid exactly five cents. It is hardly necessary to add that the identity of her runner was seldom the same for two days straight, and that a runner had to be poverty-stricken indeed before he searched among the paper nameplates downstairs and finally rang, with a disgruntled scowl, the bel of Miss Josephine Alberta Snow, Apt. 3E, who actually, had been graduated from Fisk University

What the source or size of Josephine's incom was nobody knew. Her one-room apartment, al though furnished with the same type of scarre brass bed and scratched dresser with which th other apartments were favored (for all her seve years), had received rich touches from her cul tured hands. Her walls were hung with tapestry strange pictures, china and illuminated poems. Sh had "lived well," as these things declared, and i was evident that she meant to go on "living well," Gappington Arms or no Gappington Arms.

This lady did the honors of the teacup an cookie crock each afternoon, with or without com pany. She would spread a large stool with a squar of lace, deck it with a low bowl of artificial flowers a teacup or teacups, the pot of tea, sugar, crean and lemon, and the odd-shaped crock of swee crackers.

On indoor weekdays she wore always the sam

lress—a black sateen thing that fell to her ankles ınd rose to her very chin. On the Sundays she con- lescended to go to church, she wore a pink lace, vinter and summer, which likewise embraced her rom ankle to chin. She charmed the neighborhood vith that latter get-up, too, on those summer after- ıoons when the heat drove her down from her hird-floor quarters to the little porch, with its one :hair. There she would sit, frightening everyone,)anting, fanning, and glaring at old Mr. Neville, he caretaker's eighty-two-year-old father, if he :ame out and so much as dared to look, with an :yeful of timid covetousness, at the single porch :hair over which her bottom flowed (for she was a arge lady). Then there was nothing for poor old Mr. Neville to do but sit silently on the hard stone teps—split, and crawling with ants and worse— :hew his tobacco, glance peculiarly from time to ime at that large pink lady, that pink and yellow ady, fanning indignantly at him.

As for the other tenants, they did not know what o say to Miss Snow after they had exchanged the time of day with her. Some few had attempted the tossing of sallies her way, centered in politics, the current murders, or homely philosophy, wanting to draw her out. But they very soon saw they would have to leave off all that, because it was too easy to draw her out. She would come out so far as to almost knock them down. She had a tremendous impatience with other people's ideas—unless those happened to be exactly like hers; even then, often as not, she gave hurried, almost angry, affirmative, and flew on to emphatic illuminations of her own. Then she would settle back in her chair, nod briskly a few times, as if to say, "Now! Now we are finished with it." What could be done? What was there further to be said?

24

an encounter

THEY went to the campus Jungly Hovel, a reedy-boothed place. Inside, before you saw anything, really, you got this impression of straw and reed. There were vendor outlets in the booths, and it could be observed what a struggle the management had had, trying to settle on something that was not out-and-out low, and that yet was not out-and-out highborn. In a weak moment someone had included Borden's Boogie Hoogie Woogie.

Maud Martha had gone to hear the newest

young Negro author speak, at Mandel Hall on th University campus, and whom had she run int coming out, but David McKemster. Outsid David McKemster had been talking seriously wit a tall, dignified old man. When he saw her, h gravely nodded. He gravely waved. She decided t wait for him, not knowing whether that would b agreeable to him or not. After all, this was th University world, this was his element. Perhaps h would feel she did not belong here, perhaps h would be cold to her.

He certainly was cold to her. Free of the digni fied old man, he joined her, walked with her dow Fifty-ninth Street, past the studious gray building west toward Cottage Grove. He yawned heartil at every sixth or seventh step.

"I'll put you on a streetcar," he said. "God, I'r tired."

Then nothing more was said by him, or by he —till they met a young white couple, going eas David's face lit up. These were his good, goo friends. He introduced them as such to Mau ıartha. Had they known about the panel discus-ion? No, they had not. Tell him, when had they een Mary, Mary Ehreburg? Say, he had seen Metzger Freestone tonight. Ole Metzger. (He lit a igarette.) Say, he had had dinner with the Beefy Godwins and Jane Wather this evening. Say, what were they doing tomorrow night? Well, what about going to the Adamses' tomorrow night? (He ook excited but carefully sophisticated puffs.) Yes, hey would go to the Adamses' tomorrow night. They would get Dora, and all go to the Adamses'. Say, how about going to Power's for a beer, to-night, if they had nothing else to do? Here he glanced at his companion—how to dispose of her! Well, no "how" about it, the disposal would have o be made. But first he had better buy her a cof-ee. That would pacify her. "Power'll still be up—prob'ly spr*awl*ing on that white rug of his, with Parrington in front of 'im," laughed David. It was, Maud Martha observed, one of the conceits of David McKemster that he did not have to use im-peccable English all the time. Sometimes it was permissible to make careful slips. These must be, however, when possible, sandwiched in between thick hunks of the most rational, particularistic, critical, and intellectually aloof discourse. "But first let's go to the Jungly Hovel and have coffee with Mrs. Phillips," said David McKemster.

So off to the Jungly Hovel. They went into one of the booths and ordered.

The strange young man's face was pleasant when it smiled; the jaw was a little forward; Maud Martha was reminded of Pat O'Brien, the movie star. He kept looking at her; when he looked at her his eyes were somewhat agape; "Well!" they seemed to exclaim—"Well! and what have we here!" The girl, who was his fiancée, it turned out—"Stickie"—had soft pink coloring, summer-blue eyes, was attractive. She had, her soft pink notwithstanding, that brisk, thriving, noisy, "oh-so-American" type of attractiveness. She was confidential, she communicated everything except herself, which was precisely the thing her eyes, her words, her nods, her suddenly whipped-off laughs assured you she *was* communicating. She leaned healthily across the table; her long, lovely dark hair swung at you; her bangs came right out to meet you, and her face and forefinger did too (she emphasized, robustly, some point). But herself stayed stuck to the back of her seat, and was shrewd, and "took in," and contemplated, not quite warmly, everything.

"And there was this young—man. Twenty-one or two years old, wasn't he, Maudie?" David looked down at his guest. When they sat, their heights were equal, for his length was in the legs. But he thought he was looking down at her, and she was very willing to concede that that was what he was doing, for the immediate effect of the look was to make her sit straight as a stick. "Really quite, really most a*maz*ing. Didn't you think, Maudie? Has written a book. Seems well-read chap, seems to know a lot about—a lot about—"

"Everything," supplied Maud Martha furiously.

"Well—yes." His brows gathered. He stabbed "Stickie" with a well-made gaze of seriousness, sober economy, doubt—mixed. "PRESENT things," he emphasized sharply. "He's very impressed by, he's all adither about—current plays in New York —Kafka. *That* sawt of thing," he ended. His "sawt" was not sarcastic. Our position is hardly challenged, it implied. We are still on top of the wave, it implied. We, who know about Aristotle, Plato, who weave words like anachronism, transcendentalist, cosmos, metaphysical, corollary, integer, monarchical, into our breakfast speech as a matter of course—

"And he disdains the universities!"

"Is he in school?" asked "Stickie," leaning: on the answer to that would depend—so much.

"Oh, no," David assured her, smiling. "He was pretty forceful on that point. There is nothing in the schools for *him,* he has decided. What are degrees, he asks contemptously." You see? David McKemster implied. This upstart, this, this brazen emissary, this rash representative from the ranks of the intellectual *nouveau riche*. So he was brilliant. So he could outchatter me. So intellectuality was his oyster. So he has kicked—not Parrington—but Joyce, maybe, around like a football. But he is not rooted in Aristotle, in Plato, in Aeschylus, in Epictetus. In all those Goddamn Greeks. As we are. Aloud, David skirted some of this—"Aristotle," he said, "is probably Greek to him." "Stickie" laughed quickly, stopped. Pat O'Brien smiled lazily; leered.

The waitress brought coffee, four lumps of sugar wrapped in pink paper, hot mince pie.

25

the self-solace

SONIA JOHNSON got together her towels and soap. She scrubbed out her bowls. She mixed her water.

Maud Martha, waiting, was quiet. It was pleasant to let her mind go blank. And here in the beauty shop that was not a difficult thing to do. For the perfumes in the great jars, to be sold for twelve dollars and fifty cents an ounce and one dollar a dram, or seven dollars and fifty cents an ounce and one dollar a dram, the calendars, the bright signs extolling the virtues of Lily cologne

(Made by the Management), the limp lengths of detached human hair, the pile of back-number *Vogues* and *Bazaars,* the earrings and clasps and beaded bags, white blouses—the "side line"—these things did not force themselves into the mind and make a disturbance there. One was and was not aware of them. Could sit here and think, or not think, of problems. Think, or not. One did not have to, if one wished not.

"If she burns me today—if she yanks at my hair —if she calls me sweetheart or dahlin'—"

Sonia Johnson parted the hangings that divided her reception room from her workrooms. "Come on back, baby doll."

But just then the bell tinkled, and in pushed a young white woman, wearing a Persian lamb coat, and a Persian lamb cap with black satin ribbon swirled capably in a soft knot at the back.

"Yes," thought Maud Martha, "it's legitimate. It's November. It's not cold, but it's cool. You can wear your new fur now and not be laughed at by too many people."

The young white woman introduced herself to Mrs. Johnson as Miss Ingram, and said that she had new toilet waters, a make-up base that was so good it was "practically impossible," and a new lipstick.

"No make-up bases," said Sonia. "And no toilet water. We create our own."

"This new lipstick, this new shade," Miss Ingram said, taking it out of a smart little black bag, "is just the thing for your customers. For their dark complexions."

Sonia Johnson looked interested. She always put herself out to be kind and polite to these white salesmen and saleswomen. Some beauticians were brusque. They were almost insulting. They were glad to have the whites at their mercy, if only for a few moments. They made them crawl. Then they applied the whiplash. Then they sent the poor creatures off—with no orders. Then they laughed and laughed and laughed, a terrible laughter. But Sonia Johnson was not that way. She liked to be kind and polite. She liked to be merciful. She did not like to take advantage of her power. Indeed, she felt it was better to strain, to bend far back, to spice one's listening with the smooth smile, the quick and attentive nod, the well-timed "sure" or "uh-huh." She was against this eye-for-eye-tooth-for-tooth stuff.

Maud Martha looked at Miss Ingram's beautiful legs, wondered where she got the sheer stockings that looked like bare flesh at the same time that they did not, wondered if Miss Ingram knew that in the "Negro group" there were complexions whiter than her own, and other complexions, brown, tan, yellow, cream, which could not take a dark lipstick and keep their poise. Maud Martha picked up an ancient *Vogue,* turned the pages.

"What's the lipstick's name?" Sonia Johnson asked.

"Black Beauty," Miss Ingram said, with firm-lipped determination. "You won't regret adding it to your side line, I assure you, Madam."

"What's it sell for?"

"A dollar and a half. Let me leave you—say,

ten—and in a week I'll come back and find them all gone, and you'll be here clamoring for more, I know you will. I'll leave ten."

"Well. Okay."

"That's fine, Madam. Now, I'll write down your name and address—"

Sonia rattled them off for her. Miss Ingram wrote them down. Then she closed her case.

"Now, I'll take just five dollars. Isn't that reasonable? You don't pay the rest till they're all sold. Oh, I know you're going to be just terribly pleased. And your customers too, Mrs. Johnson."

Sonia opened her cash drawer and took out five dollars for Miss Ingram. Miss Ingram brightened. The deal was closed. She pushed back a puff of straw-colored hair that had slipped from under her Persian lamb cap and fallen over the faint rose of her cheek.

"I'm mighty glad," she confided, "that the cold weather is in. I love the cold. It was awful, walking the streets in that nasty old August weather. And even September was rather close this year, didn't you think?"

Sonia agreed. "Sure was."

"People," confided Miss Ingram, "think this is a snap job. It ain't. I work like a nigger to make a few pennies. A few lousy pennies."

Maud Martha's head shot up. She did not look at Miss Ingram. She stared intently at Sonia Johnson. Sonia Johnson's sympathetic smile remained. Her eyes turned, as if magnetized, toward Maud Martha; but she forced her smile to stay on. Maud Martha went back to *Vogue*. "For," she thought, "I must have been mistaken. I was afraid I heard that woman say 'nigger.' Apparently not. Because of course Mrs. Johnson wouldn't let her get away with it. In her own shop." Maud Martha closed *Vogue*. She began to consider what she herself might have said, had she been Sonia Johnson, and had the woman really said "nigger." "I wouldn't curse. I wouldn't holler. I'll bet Mrs. Johnson would do both those things. And I could understand her wanting to, all right. I would be gentle in a cold way. I would give her, not a return insult—directly, at any rate!—but information. I would get it across to her that—" Maud Martha stretched. "But I wouldn't insult her." Maud Martha began to take the hairpins out of her hair. "I'm glad, though, that she didn't say it. She's pretty and pleasant. If she had said it, I would feel all strained and tied up inside, and I would feel that it was my duty to help Mrs. Johnson get it settled, to help clear it up in some way. I'm too relaxed to fight today. Sometimes fighting is interesting. Today, it would have been just plain old ugly duty."

"Well, I wish you success with Black Beauty," Miss Ingram said, smiling in a tired manner, as she buttoned the top button of her Persian lamb. She walked quickly out of the door. The little bell tinkled charmingly.

Sonia Johnson looked at her customer with thoughtful narrowed eyes. She walked over, dragged a chair up close. She sat. She began to speak in a dull level tone.

"You know, why I didn't catch her up on that,

is—our people is got to stop feeling so sensitive about these words like 'nigger' and such. I often think about this, and how these words like 'nigger' don't mean to some of these here white people what our people *think* they mean. Now, 'nigger,' for instance, means to them something bad, or slavey-like, or low. They don't mean anything against me. I'm a Negro, not a 'nigger.' Now, a white man can be a 'nigger,' according to their meaning for the word, just like a colored man can. So why should I go getting all stepped up about a thing like that? Our people is got to stop getting all stepped up about every little thing, especially when it don't amount to nothing. . . ."

"You mean to say," Maud Martha broke in, "that that woman really did say 'nigger'?"

"Oh, yes, she said it, all right, but like I'm telling—"

"Well! At first, I thought she said it, but then I decided I must have been mistaken, because you weren't getting after her."

"Now that's what I'm trying to explain to you,

dearie. Sure, I could have got all hot and bothered, and told her to clear out of here, or cussed her daddy, or something like that. But what would be the point, when, like I say, that word 'nigger' can mean one of them just as fast as one of us, and in fact it don't mean us, and in fact we're just too sensitive and all? What would be the point? Why make enemies? Why go getting all hot and bothered all the time?"

Maud Martha stared steadily into Sonia Johnson's irises. She said nothing. She kept on staring into Sonia Johnson's irises.

26

Maud Martha's tumor

AS she bent over Paulette, she felt a peculiar pain in her middle, at the right. She touched the spot. There it was. A knot, hard, manipulable, the proscription of her doom.

At first, she could only be weak (as the pain grew sharper and sharper). Then she was aware of creeping fear; fear of the operating table, the glaring instruments, the cold-faced nurses, the relentlessly submerging ether, the chokeful awakening, the pain, the ensuing cancer, the ensuing death.

Then she thought of her life. Decent childhood, happy Christmases; some shreds of romance, a marriage, pregnancy and the giving birth, her growing child, her experiments in sewing, her books, her conversations with her friends and enemies.

"It hasn't been bad," she thought.

"It's been interesting," she thought, as she put Paulette in the care of Mrs. Maxawanda Barksdale and departed for the doctor's.

She looked at the trees, she looked at the grass, she looked at the faces of the passers-by. It had been interesting, it had been rather good, and it was still rather good. But really, she was ready. Since the time had come, she was ready. Paulette would miss her for a long time, Paul for less, but really, their sorrow was their business, not hers. Her business was to descend into the deep cool, the salving dark, to be alike indifferent to the good and the not-good.

"And what," asked Dr. Williams, "did you do yesterday that was out of line with your regular routine?" He mashed her here, tapped there.

She remembered.

"Why, I was doing the bends."

"Doing—"

"The bends. Exercising. With variations. I lay on the bed, also, and keeping my upper part absolutely still, I raised my legs up, then lowered them, twenty times."

"Is this a nightly custom of yours?"

"No. Last night was the first time I had done it since before my little girl was born."

"Three dollars, please."

"You mean—I'm not going to die."

She bounced down the long flight of tin-edged stairs, was shortly claimed by the population, which seemed proud to have her back. An old woman, bent, shriveled, smiled sweetly at her.

She was already on South Park. She jumped in a jitney and went home.

27

Paul in the 011 Club

THE 011 Club did not like it so much, your buying only a beer. . . .

Do you want to get into the war? Maud Martha "thought at" Paul, as, over their wine, she watched his eye-light take leave of her. To get into the war, perhaps. To be mixed up in peculiar, hooped adventure, adventure dominant, entire, ablaze with bunched and fidgeting color, pageantry, thrilling with the threat of danger—through which he would come without so much as a bruised ankle.

The baby was getting darker all the time! She knew that he was tired of his wife, tired of his living quarters, tired of working at Sam's, tired of his two suits.

He is ever so tired, she thought.

He had no money, no car, no clothes, and he had not been put up for membership in the Foxy Cats Club.

Something should happen. He was not on show. She knew that he believed he had been born to invade, to occur, to confront, to inspire the flapping of flags, to panic people. To wear, but carelessly, a crown. What could give him his chance, illuminate his gold?—be a happening?

She looked about, about at these, the people he would like to impress. The real people. It was Sunday afternoon and they were dressed in their best. It was May, and for hats the women wore gardens and birds. They wore tight-fitting prints, or flounced satin, or large-flowered silk under the coats they could not afford but bought anyhow. Their hair was intricately curled, or it was sedately marcelled. Some of it was hennaed. Their escorts were in broad-shouldered suits, and sported dapper handkerchiefs. Their hair was either slicked back or very close-cut. All spoke in subdued tones. There were no roughnecks here. These people knew what whiskies were good, what wine was "the thing" with this food, that food, what places to go, how to dance, how to smoke, how much stress to put on love, how to dress, when to curse, and did not indulge (for the most part) in homosexuality but could discuss it without eagerness, distaste, curiosity—without anything but ennui. These, in her husband's opinion, were the real people. And this was the real place. The manner of the waitresses toward the patrons, by unspoken agreement, was just this side of insulting. They seemed to have something to prove. They wanted you to know, to be *sure* that they were as good as you were and maybe a lot better. They did not want you to be misled by the fact that on a Sunday afternoon, instead of silk and little foxes, they wore white uniforms and carried trays and picked up (rapidly) tips.

A flame-colored light flooded the ceiling in the dining foyer. (But there was a blue-red-purple note in the bar.) On the east wall of the dining foyer, painted against a white background, was an unclothed lady, with a careless bob, challenging nipples, teeth-revealing smile; her arms were lifted, to call attention to "all"—and she was standing behind a few huge leaves of sleepy color and amazing design. On the south wall was painted one of those tropical ladies clad in carefully careless sarong, and bearing upon her head with great ease and glee a platter of fruit—apples, spiky pineapple, bananas. . . .

She watched the little dreams of smoke as they spiraled about his hand, and she thought about happenings. She was afraid to suggest to him that, to most people, nothing at all "happens." That most people merely live from day to day until they die. That, after he had been dead a year, doubtless fewer than five people would think of him oftener than once a year. That there might even come a year when no one on earth would think of him at all.

28

brotherly love

MAUD MARTHA was fighting with a chicken. The nasty, nasty mess. It had been given a bitter slit with the bread knife and the bread knife had been biting in that vomit-looking interior for almost five minutes without being able to detach certain resolute parts from their walls. The bread knife had it all to do, as Maud Martha had no intention of putting her hand in there. Another hack—another hack—STUFF! Splat in her eye. She leaped at the faucet.

She thought she had praise coming to her. Sh
was doing this job with less stomach-curving tha
ever before. She thought of the times before th
war, when there were more chickens than peopl
wanting to buy them, and butchers were happ
to clean them, and even cut them up. None of tha
now. In those happy, happy days—if she ha
opened up a chicken and seen it all unsightly lik
this, and smelled it all smelly, she would hav
scooped up the whole batch of slop and rushed i
to the garbage can. Now meat was jewelry and sh
was practically out of Red Points. You were luck
to find a chicken. She had to be as brave as sh
could.

People could do this! people could cut a chicke
open, take out the mess, with bare hands or
bread knife, pour water in, as in a bag, pour wate
out, shake the corpse by neck or by legs, free th
straggles of water. Could feel that insinuating slip-
ping bone, survey that soft, that headless death
The *faint*hearted could do it. But if the chicke
were a man!—cold man with no head or feet an

with all the little feath—er, hairs to be pulled, and the intestines loosened and beginning to ooze out, and the gizzard yet to be grabbed and the stench beginning to rise! And yet the chicken was a sort of person, a respectable individual, with its own kind of dignity. The difference was in the knowing. What was unreal to you, you could deal with violently. If chickens were ever to be safe, people would have to live with them, and know them, see them loving their children, finishing the evening meal, arranging jealousy.

When the animal was ready for the oven Maud Martha smacked her lips at the thought of her meal.

29

millinery

"LOOKS lovely on you," said the manager. "Makes you look—" What? Beautiful? Charming? Glamorous? Oh no, oh no, she could not stoop to the usual lies; not today; her coffee had been too strong, had not set right; and there had been another fight at home, for her daughter continued to insist on gallivanting about with that Greek—a Greek!—not even a Jew, which, though revolting enough, was at least becoming fashionable, wa "timely." Oh, not today would she cater to these nigger women who tried on every hat in her shop, who used no telling what concoctions of smelly grease on the heads that integrity, straightforwardness, courage, would certainly have kept kinky. She started again—"Makes you look—" She stopped.

"How much is the hat?" Maud Martha asked.

"Seven ninety-nine."

Maud Martha rose, went to the door.

"Wait, wait," called the hat woman, hurrying after her. She smiled at Maud Martha. When she looked at Maud Martha, it was as if God looked; it was as if—

"Now just how much, Madam, had you thought you would prefer to pay?"

"Not a cent over five."

"Five? Five, dearie? You expect to buy a hat like this for five dollars? This, this straw that you can't even get any more and which I showed you only because you looked like a lady of taste who could appreciate a good value?"

"Well," said Maud Martha, "thank you." She opened the door.

"Wait, wait," shrieked the hat woman. Good-naturedly, the escaping customer hesitated again. "Just a moment," ordered the hat woman coldly. "I'll speak to the—to the owner. He might be willing to make some slight reduction, since you're an old customer. I remember you. You've been in here several times, haven't you?"

"I've never been in the store before." The woman rushed off as if she had heard nothing. She rushed off to consult with the owner. She rushed off to appeal to the boxes in the back room.

Presently the hat woman returned.

"Well. The owner says it'll be a crying shame, but seeing as how you're such an old customer he'll make a reduction. He'll let you have it for five. Plus tax, of course!" she added chummily; they had, always, more appreciation when, after one of these "reductions," you added that.

"I've decided against the hat."

"What? Why, you told— But, you said—"

Maud Martha went out, tenderly closed the door.

"Black—oh, black—" said the hat woman to her hats—which, on the slender stands, shone pink and blue and white and lavender, showed off their tassels, their sleek satin ribbons, their veils, their flower coquettes.

30

at the Burns-Coopers'

IT was a little red and white and black woman who appeared in the doorway of the beautiful house in Winnetka.

About, thought Maud Martha, thirty-four.

"I'm Mrs. Burns-Cooper," said the woman, "and after this, well, it's all right this time, because it's your first time, but after this time always use the back entrance."

There is a pear in my icebox, and one end of rye

bread. Except for three Irish potatoes and a cup of flour and the empty Christmas boxes, there is absolutely nothing on my shelf. My husband is laid off. There is newspaper on my kitchen table instead of oilcloth. I can't find a filing job in a hurry. I'll smile at Mrs. Burns-Cooper and hate her just some.

"First, you have the beds to make," said Mrs. Burns-Cooper. "You either change the sheets or air the old ones for ten minutes. I'll tell you about the changing when the time comes. It isn't any special day. You are to pull my sheets, and pat and pat and pull till all's tight and smooth. Then shake the pillows into the slips, carefully. Then punch them in the middle.

"Next, there is the washing of the midnight snack dishes. Next, there is the scrubbing. Now, I know that your other ladies have probably wanted their floors scrubbed after dinner. I'm different. I like to enjoy a bright clean floor all the day. You can just freshen it up a little before you leave in the evening, if it needs a few more touches. Another thing. I disapprove of mops. You can do a better job on your knees.

"Next is dusting. Next is vacuuming—that's for Tuesdays and Fridays. On Wednesdays, ironing and silver cleaning.

"Now about cooking. You're very fortunate in that here you have only the evening meal to prepare. Neither of us has breakfast, and I always step out for lunch. Isn't that lucky?"

"It's quite a kitchen, isn't it?" Maud Martha observed. "I mean, big."

Mrs. Burns-Cooper's brows raced up in amazement.

"Really? I hadn't thought so. I'll bet"—she twinkled indulgently—"you're comparing it to your *own* little kitchen." And why do that, her light eyes laughed. Why talk of beautiful mountains and grains of alley sand in the same breath?

"Once," mused Mrs. Burns-Cooper, "I had a girl who botched up the kitchen. Made a botch out of it. But all I had to do was just sort of cock my head and say, 'Now, now, Albertine!' Her name was Albertine. Then she'd giggle and scrub and scrub and she was *so* sorry about trying to take advantage."

It was while Maud Martha was peeling potatoes for dinner that Mrs. Burns-Cooper laid herself out to prove that she was not a snob. Then it was that Mrs. Burns-Cooper came out to the kitchen and, sitting, talked and talked at Maud Martha. In my college days. At the time of my debut. The imported lace on my lingerie. My brother's rich wife's Stradivarius. When I was in Madrid. The charm of the Nile. Cost fifty dollars. Cost one hundred dollars. Cost one thousand dollars. Shall I mention, considered Maud Martha, my own social triumphs, my own education, my travels to Gary and Milwaukee and Columbus, Ohio? Shall I mention my collection of fancy pink satin bras? She decided against it. She went on listening, in silence, to the confidences until the arrival of the lady's mother-in-law (large-eyed, strong, with hair of a mighty white, and with an eloquent, angry bosom). Then the junior Burns-Cooper was very much the mistress, was stiff, cool, authoritative.

There was no introduction, but the elder Burns-Cooper boomed, "Those potato parings are entirely too thick!"

The two of them, richly dressed, and each with that health in the face that bespeaks, or seems to bespeak, much milk drinking from earliest childhood, looked at Maud Martha. There was no remonstrance; no firing! They just looked. But for the first time, she understood what Paul endured daily. For so—she could gather from a Paul-word here, a Paul-curse there—his Boss! when, squared, upright, terribly upright, superior to the President, commander of the world, he wished to underline Paul's lacks, to indicate soft shock, controlled incredulity. As his boss looked at Paul, so these people looked at her. As though she were a child, a ridiculous one, and one that ought to be given a little shaking, except that shaking was—not quite the thing, would not quite do. One held up one's finger (if one did anything), cocked one's head, was arch. As in the old song, one hinted, "Tut tut! now now! come come!" Metal rose, all built, in one's eye.

I'll never come back, Maud Martha assured herself, when she hung up her apron at eight in the evening. She knew Mrs. Burns-Cooper would be puzzled. The wages were very good. Indeed, what could be said in explanation? Perhaps that the hours were long. I couldn't explain *my* explanation, she thought.

One walked out from that almost perfect wall, spitting at the firing squad. What difference did it make whether the firing squad understood or did not understand the manner of one's retaliation or why one had to retaliate?

Why, one was a human being. One wore clean nightgowns. One loved one's baby. One drank cocoa by the fire—or the gas range—come the evening, in the wintertime.

31

on Thirty-fourth Street

MAUD MARTHA went east on Thirty-fourth Street, headed for Cottage Grove. It was August, and Thirty-fourth Street was all in bloom. The blooms, in their undershirts, sundresses and diapers, were hanging over porches and fence stiles and strollers, and were even bringing chairs out to the rims of the sidewalks.

At the corner of Thirty-fourth and Cottage Grove, a middle-aged blind man on a three-legged stool picked at a scarred guitar. The five or six patched and middle-aged men around him sang in husky, low tones, which carried the higher tone—ungarnished, insistent, at once a question and an answer—of the instrument.

Those men were going no further—and had gone nowhere. Tragedy.

She considered that word. On the whole, she felt, life was more comedy than tragedy. Nearly everything that happened had its comic element, not too well buried, either. Sooner or later one could find something to laugh at in almost every situation. That was what, in the last analysis, could keep folks from going mad. The truth was, if you got a good Tragedy out of a lifetime, one good, ripping tragedy, thorough, unridiculous, bottom-scraping, *not* the issue of human stupidity, you were doing, she thought, very well, you were doing well.

32

Mother comes to call

MAMA came, bringing two oranges, nine pecans, a Hershey bar and a pear.

Mama explained that one of the oranges was for Maud Martha, one was for Paulette. The Hershey bar was for Paulette. The pear was for Maud Martha, for it was not, Mama said, a very good pear. Four of the pecans were for Maud Martha, four were for Paulette, one was for Paul.

Maud Martha spread her little second-hand table—a wide tin band was wound beneath the top, for strength—with her finest wedding gift, a really good white luncheon cloth. She brought out white coffee cups and saucers, sugar, milk, and a little pink pot of cocoa. She brought a plate of frosted gingerbread. Mother and daughter sat down to Tea.

"And how is Helen? I haven't seen her in two weeks. When I'm over there to see you, she's always out."

"Helen doesn't like to come here much," said Mama, nodding her head over the gingerbread. "Not enough cinnamon in this but very good. She says it sort of depresses her. She wants you to have more things."

"I like nutmeg better than cinnamon. I have a lot of things. I have more than she has. I have a husband, a nice little girl, and a clean home of my own."

"A kitchenette of your own," corrected Mama, "without even a private bathroom. I think Paul could do a little better, Maud Martha."

"It's hard to find even a kitchenette."

"Nothing beats a trial but a failure. Helen thinks she's going to marry Doctor Williams."

"Our own family doctor. Not our own family doctor!"

"She says her mind's about made up."

"But he's over fifty years old."

"She says he's steady, not like the young ones she knows, and kind, and will give her a decent home."

"And what do you say?"

"I say, it's a hard cold world and a woman had better do all she can to help herself get along as long as what she does is honest. It isn't as if she didn't like Doctor Williams."

"She always did, yes. Ever since we were children, and he used to bring her licorice sticks, and forgot to bring any to me, except very seldom."

"It isn't as if she merely sold herself. She'll try to make him happy, I'm sure. Helen was always a good girl. And in any marriage, the honeymoon is soon over."

"What does Papa say?"

"He's thinking of changing doctors."

"It hasn't been a hard cold world for you, Mama. You've been very lucky. You've had a faithful, homecoming husband, who bought you a house, not the best house in town, but a house. You have, most of the time, plenty to eat, you have enough clothes so that you can always be clean. And you're strong as a horse."

"It certainly has been a hard season," said Belva Brown. "I don't know when we've had to burn so much coal in October before."

"I'm thinking of Helen."

"What about Helen, dear?"

"It's funny how some people are just charming, just pretty, and others, born of the same parents, are just not."

"You've always been wonderful, dear."

They looked at each other.

"I always say you make the best cocoa in the family."

"I'm never going to tell my secret."

"That girl down at the corner, next to the parsonage—you know?—is going to have another baby."

"The third? And not her husband's *either*?"

"Not her husband's either."

"Did Mrs. Whitfield get all right?"

"No, she'll have to have the operation."

33

tree leaves leaving trees

AIRPLANES and games and dolls and books and wagons and blackboards and boats and guns and bears and rabbits and pandas and ducks, and dogs and cats and gray elephants with black howdahs and rocking chairs and houses and play dishes and scooters and animal hassocks, and trains and trucks and yo-yos and telephones and balls and jeeps and jack-in-the-boxes and puzzles and rocking horses.

And Santa Claus.

Round, ripe, rosy,
As the stories said.
And white, it fluffed out from his chin,
It laughed about his head.

And there were the children. Many groups of them, for this was a big department store. Santa pushed out plump ho-ho-ho's! He patted the children's cheeks, and if a curl was golden and sleek enough he gave it a bit of a tug, and sometimes he gave its owner a bit of a hug. And the children's Christmas wants were almost torn out of them.

It was very merry and much as the children had dreamed.

Now came little Paulette. When the others had been taken care of. Her insides scampering like mice. And, leaving her eyeballs, diamonds and stars.

Santa Claus.

Suddenly she was shy.

Maud Martha smiled, gave her a tiny shove, spoke as much to Santa Claus as to her daughter.

"Go on. There he is. You've wanted to talk to him all this time. Go on. Tell Santa what you want for Christmas."

"No."

Another smile, another shove, with some impatience, with some severity in it. And Paulette was off.

"Hello!"

Santa Claus rubbed his palms together and looked vaguely out across the Toy Department.

He was unable to see either mother or child.

"I want," said Paulette, "a wagon, a doll, a big ball, a bear and a tricycle with a horn."

"Mister," said Maud Martha, "my little girl is talking to you."

Santa Claus's neck turned with hard slowness, carrying his unwilling face with it.

"Mister," said Maud Martha.

"And what—do you want for Christmas." No question mark at the end.

"I want a wagon, a doll, a bear, a big ball, and a tricycle with a horn."

Silence. Then, "Oh." Then, "Um-hm."

Santa Claus had taken care of Paulette.

"And some candy and some nuts and a seesaw and bow and arrow."

"Come on, baby."

"But I'm not through, Mama."

"Santa Claus is through, hon."

Outside, there was the wonderful snow, high and heavy, crusted with blue twinkles. The air was quiet.

"Certainly is a nice night," confided Mama.

"Why didn't Santa Claus like me?"

"Baby, of course he liked you."

"He didn't like me. Why didn't he like me?"

"It maybe seemed that way to you. He has a lot on his mind, of course."

"He liked the other children. He smiled at them and shook their hands."

"He maybe got tired of smiling. Sometimes even I get—"

"He didn't look at me, he didn't shake *my* hand."

"Listen, child. People don't have to kiss you to show they like you. Now you know Santa Claus liked you. What have I been telling you? Santa Claus loves every child, and on the night before Christmas he brings them swell presents. Don't you remember, when you told Santa Claus you wanted the ball and bear and tricycle and doll he said 'Um-hm'? That meant he's going to bring you all those. You watch and see. Christmas'll be here in a few days. You'll wake up Christmas morning and find them and then you'll know Santa Claus loved *you too.*"

Helen, she thought, would not have twitched, back there. Would not have yearned to jerk trimming scissors from purse and jab jab jab that evading eye. Would have gathered her fires, patted them, rolled them out, and blown on them. Because it really would not have made much difference to Helen. Paul would have twitched, twitched awfully, might have cursed, but after the first tough cough-up of rage would forget, or put off studious perusal indefinitely.

She could neither resolve nor dismiss. There were these scraps of baffled hate in her, hate with no eyes, no smile and—this she especially regretted, called her hungriest lack—not much voice.

Furtively, she looked down at Paulette. Was Paulette believing her? Surely she was not going to begin to think tonight, to try to find out answers tonight. She hoped the little creature wasn't ready. She hoped there hadn't been enough for that. She wasn't up to coping with— Some other night, not tonight.

Feeling her mother's peep, Paulette turned her face upward. Maud Martha wanted to cry.

Keep her that land of blue!

Keep her those fairies, with witches always killed at the end, and Santa every winter's lord, kind, sheer being who never perspires, who never does or says a foolish or ineffective thing, who never looks grotesque, who never has occasion to pull the chain and flush the toilet.

34

back from the wars!

THERE was Peace, and her brother Harry was back from the wars, and well.

And it was such a beautiful day!

The weather was bidding her bon voyage.

She did not have to tip back the shade of her little window to know that outside it was bright, because the sunshine had broken through the dark green of that shade and was glorifying every bit of her room. And the air crawling in at the half-inch crack was like a feather, and it tickled her throat, it teased her lashes, it made her sit up in bed and stretch, and zip the dark green shade up to the very top of the window—and made her whisper What, *what*, am I to do with all of this life?

And exactly what was one to do with it all? At a moment like this one was ready for anything, was not afraid of anything. If one were down in a dark cool valley one could stick arms out and presto they would be wings cutting away at the higher layers of air. At a moment like this one could think even of death with a sharp exhilaration, feel that death was a part of life: that life was good and death would be good too.

Maud Martha, with her daughter, got out-of-doors.

She did not need information, or solace, or a guidebook, or a sermon—not in this sun!—not in this blue air!

. . . They "marched," they battled behind her brain—the men who had drunk beer with the best of them, the men with two arms off and two legs *back from the wars!*

off, the men with the parts of faces. Then her guts divided, then her eyes swam under frank mist.

And the Negro press (on whose front pages beamed the usual representations of womanly Beauty, pale and pompadoured) carried the stories of the latest of the Georgia and Mississippi lynchings. . . .

But the sun was shining, and some of the people in the world had been left alive, and it was doubtful whether the ridiculousness of man would ever completely succeed in destroying the world—or, in fact, the basic equanimity of the least and commonest flower: for would its kind not come up again in the spring? come up, if necessary, among, between, or out of—beastly inconvenient!—the smashed corpses lying in strict composure, in that hush infallible and sincere.

And was not this something to be thankful for?

And, in the meantime, while people did live they would be grand, would be glorious and brave, would have nimble hearts that would beat and beat. They would even get up nonsense, through wars, through divorce, through evictions and jiltings and taxes.

And, in the meantime, she was going to have another baby.

The weather was bidding her bon voyage.

Set in Intertype Baskerville
Format by Marguerite Swanton
Manufactured by the Haddon Craftsmen, Inc.
Published by HARPER & BROTHERS, *New York*